Praise for the Aurora Teagarden novels by

Charlaine Harris

"Roe Teagarden is as capable and potentially complex as P. D. James's Cordelia Gray."
—*Publishers Weekly*

"Roe is so charming you will want to go back and read the first three."
—*Mostly Murder*

"The author's brisk, upbeat style keeps tension simmering under the everyday surface."
—*Publishers Weekly*

"Good reading, augmented by solid characterization and occasional humor."
—*Library Journal*

"Charlaine Harris is a talented writer."
—*Washington Post Book World*

"Harris has down pat the laid-back atmosphere, country friendliness, and occasional sordid secrets of [the] small-town South."
—*Arkansas Democrat Gazette*

Charlaine Harris

Last Scene Alive

MIRA

ISBN-13: 978-0-7783-2364-8
ISBN-10: 0-7783-2364-1

LAST SCENE ALIVE

ACKNOWLEDGMENTS

Many people gave me information I used or misused in this book. First and foremost was Tom Smith, who knows more about the movie industry than I could ever include in one book. Also of great help were William Peschel, who gave me a great account of his time spent as an extra; Dr. John Alexander, who never minds answering odd questions; and Donna Moore, one of my cyberfriends on DorothyL, who gave me the title for this book.

One

When I stopped at the end of the driveway to extract my letters and magazines from the mailbox, I never imagined that in five minutes I'd be sitting at my kitchen table reading an article about myself. But my entertainment magazine had had a fascinating teaser on the cover: "Crusoe's Book Comes to the Screen (Finally)—WHIMSICAL MURDERS Goes On Location." It had taken me only seconds to flip pages to the article, which was faced by a full-page picture of my former friend Robin Crusoe, his long frame folded into a chair behind a desk piled high with books. Then, with a much deeper sensation of shock, I realized that, in a green-shaded sidebar, the small woman walking to her car, head down, was me. Not surprisingly, I decided to read the sidebar first.

"It was a strangely jolting experience to see Aurora Teagarden in the flesh," began the writer, one Marjory Bolton.

Strangely jolting, my tushy.

"The diminutive librarian, whose courage and perspicuity led to the discovery of the serial killers terrorizing Lawrenceton, Georgia, is no recluse."

Why would I be?

"Though only in her thirties, she's experienced more excitement than most women have in their lifetimes," I read, "and though she became a widow last November, Aurora Teagarden could pass for someone ten years her junior." Well, I kind of liked that. I could see the end of my thirties if I looked real hard. I wasn't looking.

"She comes to work at the Lawrenceton Library every day, driving her new Chevy." Would I drive someone else's? "Modest in dress and demeanor, Teagarden hardly appears to be the independently wealthy woman she is." Why would I wear designer originals (an inexplicable waste of money anyway) to my job at the library? This was absurdity.

I skimmed the remaining paragraphs, hoping to see something that made sense. Actually, I wouldn't have minded another reference to my youthful appearance. But no. "Though Teagarden refused to let the filmmakers use her name, the main female character in the script is widely held to be based on her persona. Teagarden's mother, Aida Queensland, a multi-million-dollar real estate salesperson, attributes her daughter's distancing herself from the project to Teagarden's aversion to the memories the incidents left and to Teagarden's deeply religious heritage."

I brought the cordless phone into the kitchen and hit an auto-dial number. "Mother, did you tell this Marjory Bolton that I came from a 'deeply religious heritage'?" We hadn't even settled on the Episcopal Church until Mother had married John Queensland.

My mother had the grace to sound a little embarrassed as she said, "Good evening, Aurora. She asked me if we went to church, and I said yes."

I read through the paragraph again. "And you told her you were a multi-million-dollar real estate broker?"

"Well, I am. And I thought I might as well get in a plug for the business."

"Like you needed it!"

"Business could always be better. Besides, I'm trying to get into the best position for selling the firm. One of these days I'm going to retire."

It wasn't the first time in the past couple of months Mother had said something about selling Select Realty. Since John had had a heart attack, my mother had cut back on her work hours. Apparently, she'd also begun to think about how much longer she wanted to work.

Two years ago, I'd have sworn she'd die while she was showing a house, but now I knew better. She'd gotten a wake-up call.

"Listen to this," I said. "Ms. Teagarden, close friend of rising power-that-be Cartland Sewell, may have political plans. Some insiders regard her as a power behind the scenes in area politics." Who on earth could've told them that? What a bunch of..."

"Aurora!" Mother warned.

"Codswallop," I finished. It was a word I'd never had occasion to say out loud before.

"I'm sure it was Bubba himself," Mother said. She was more politically astute without trying than I would be if I had a fully briefed advisor.

"Really?" Even I could hear the wonderment in my voice.

She sighed. "I hope you never remotely consider running for office or backing any candidate you really want to win," she advised me. "And I've got to try to remember to call him Cartland. After calling him Bubba for forty years, Cartland is a mouthful. He seems to think he has a better chance of getting elected if he goes by his christened name."

Well, I might not be politically astute like Bubba Sewell—excuse me, *Cartland* Sewell—but I could see that even my own mother had had a self-serving reason for contributing a quote to a completely unwanted, unnecessary magazine article about me.

"Have you finished the whole article?" Mother asked, and her voice had taken on some anxiety.

"No." That sounded ominous. I skipped over the last part of the sidebar, the part where my friend Angel Youngblood had shoved the photographer, and returned to the main body of the article, the reason for the revival of interest in yours truly.

"After a long and frustrating wait, the grisly tale of the murders upon which Robin Crusoe's book WHIM-

SICAL DEATH was based is coming to the small screen as a two-part miniseries. Filmmakers hope for a more successful pairing of true-crime book and movie than *Midnight in the Garden of Good and Evil*. Crusoe's sojourn in Hollywood has made him skeptical of the result. "I don't know how the natives of Lawrenceton will feel about the job we're doing," Crusoe admitted. "I plan to be there for the location shoot." Crusoe has another reason to be on the scene; he's the constant companion of actress Celia Shaw, who will play the Teagarden character."

I flipped the page, just hoping. Yep, there it was—a small shot of Robin and Celia Shaw at some movie premiere party. Celia had done an Emmy-winning guest stint on *ER* as a sexually addicted med student, and in this picture she and Robin were whooping it up with three of the cast members. My mouth dropped open. It was one thing to have known for the past several years that Robin was in Hollywood, writing his mystery novels from there while he touted the screenplay of his book, but it was another thing entirely to see him being Hollywood.

I examined Celia Shaw's face, the size of a fingernail, with a fascination I found hard to explain to myself. Of course, she really didn't look much like me, even like the Aurora of a few years ago. She was short, and she had notable cleavage, and her eyes were brown; those were the only points of similarity. Her face was narrower, her lips were plumper, and she had more of a nose. (I could hardly be said to have a nose at all.) And, of course, she wasn't wearing glasses. She was wearing a dress I wouldn't even have given a second glance to as I flicked through a rack. It was deep emerald green, had a sequined top, and plunged low.

I glanced down at my own cleavage, modestly covered by the tobacco brown twin set I'd worn to work over khakis. I'd look good in that dress (I told myself loyally), but I'd be uncomfortable the entire time.

Not that I could imagine going to any occasion where that dress would be appropriate. A few Lawrencetonians mixed in Atlanta society, as our small town came closer and closer to being absorbed in the urban sprawl of the South's great city, but I was not one of them; nor had I ever wanted to be.

I'd never really enjoyed the social functions I had to attend or arrange as Martin's wife, and they'd been relatively modest. As the head of the large Pan-Am Agra plant, Martin had had many obligations, only some of them related to actually running the plant.

When I looked back on the two years we'd been married, the evenings seemed a blur of entertaining higher-ups from out of town, potential customers, and representatives from the bigger accounts. We'd been invited to every charity event in Lawrenceton, and not a few in Atlanta. I'd bought the appropriate clothes, worn them, and smiled through it all, but those social evenings hadn't been much fun. Coming home with Martin had been the good part.

Coming home with Martin had been worth every minute of that social tedium.

And with that memory, the heaviness I carried inside me every moment of every day came crashing back down. I actually felt the misery descend.

Until I'd thought about the article, been distracted for a few minutes, I hadn't realized how grievous a burden I was carrying: it was the weight of my widowhood.

As abruptly as it had engaged my interest, the magazine article repelled me. There would be strangers swarming around my hometown, strangers who were interested in me without caring about me. All the horror of those old deaths would be raked up. At least a few townspeople would be made miserable, as the deaths of their loved ones were reenacted for the titillation of whomever had a television set. There was no way to stop this from happening, apparently—no way to keep the curtain of privacy drawn around me. Already, in a national magazine, I was being depicted as mysterious, odd, and somewhat boring.

I didn't want this movie to be made, and I didn't want those people here.

As I'd thought, there were a few people in Lawrenceton who were as glum as I was over the prospect of entertaining a film company. One of them was the aforementioned Bubba—excuse me, Cartland—Sewell's wife, my friend Lizanne. Her parents were among the victims of the pair of serial killers who had caused us all tremendous grief. Lizanne, too, had read the magazine article, I discovered later that evening.

Lizanne said, "Roe, I imagine Bubba's boosterism got in the way of his common sense." Beautiful Lizanne has always been a tranquil woman, resolutely uninvolved in any town intrigues, and for the past two years her attention had been narrowly focused on her children, two boys she'd named Brandon and Davis. Brandon was eighteen months old, and Davis had just turned three months, so Lizanne had her hands full. In the course of our choppy telephone conversation, we were constantly interrupted. Bubba, Lizanne told me, was at a bar association meeting. I fumed at not being able to speak my mind to Bubba, but I would have settled for a nice chat with Lizanne. But in five minutes, Brandon's shrieking and the wails of the baby reached such a peak that Lizanne excused herself.

While I washed my few dishes that cool October evening, I found myself wondering which of the unfamiliar faces in the library in recent weeks had belonged to the magazine writer. You'd think a writer for an L.A.-based entertainment weekly would have stood out like a sore thumb in our library. But the dress of our culture has become so universal, it isn't as easy to spot outsiders as it used to be.

It struck me as particularly nasty that this woman had been able to come and stare at me and dissect me, while I'd been totally unaware. She'd said I'd turned down a request for an interview. That was so automatic that I actually might not have remembered it. But how could I have been oblivious to the fact that I was under observation? I must have been even more preoccupied than I'd thought.

Being a widow was a full-time occupation, at least emotionally.

Everyone (that is, my mother and her husband John, and most of my friends) had expected me to move back into town after my husband's death. Our house, a gift to me from Martin when we'd married, was a little isolated, and too large for one person. But from my point of view, I'd loved the man and I loved my home. I couldn't lose both at once.

So I stayed in the house that had been known for years as the Julius house. When Martin had given it to me, I'd renovated it from the bottom up, and I kept it up well, though now I had to have more help in that keeping. Shelby Youngblood, Angel's husband and a close friend of my husband's, had offered to come out and do the mowing, but I'd turned him down gently. I knew Shelby, with his own yard and house and baby, had plenty to do when he had a couple of days off work. I'd hired a yard service to do most of the heavier work, but every now and then I got out and put in bedding plants, or trimmed the roses.

With less justification than the yard service, I'd also hired a maid. Martin had always wanted me to have help in the house, but I'd felt perfectly capable of taking care of the house and cooking, though I was working at least part-time most of our marriage. Now, oddly, I was seized with the determination that the house should always look immaculate. It was as if I was going to show it to a prospective buyer any moment. I had even cleaned out all the closets. Where my new passion for absolute order and cleanliness had come from, why it possessed me, I could not tell you. The maid (whose identity kept changing—at the moment it was a heavy older woman named Catherine Quick) came in once a week and did all the heavy cleaning— the bathrooms, the kitchen, the dusting, and the vacuuming—while I did everything else. I didn't suffer a smudge on the kitchen floor or an unwashed sock. Even though only one upstairs bedroom, the downstairs study, one bathroom, and the kitchen were in any kind of regular use, I kept this regimen up month after month.

I guess I was a little crazy: or, since I could afford a slightly kinder word, eccentric.

As I trudged up the stairs to go to bed that night, I wondered, for the first time, if keeping the house hadn't been a mistake.

Opening the bedroom door still gave me a little shock. One thing I *had* changed, a couple of months after Martin died, was our bedroom. Once fairly masculine and centered around the king-sized bed, now the big room was peach and ivory and fawn, the bed was a queen, and the furniture was more ornate. Atop the chest of drawers, there was a picture of Martin and me at our wedding. That picture was all that was bearable.

I looked at it for a long moment as I pulled off my rings and put them in a pile in front of the frame. I added my watch to the little heap before I climbed into the high bed and switched on the lamp, stretching a little further to reach the switch to flick off the overhead light. I picked up the book I was reading (though for months I hadn't remembered a word of any book I read) and had completed just a page when the telephone rang. I glanced at the clock and frowned.

"Yes?" I said curtly into the receiver.

"Roe?" The voice was familiar, tentative and masculine.

"Who is this?" I asked.

"Ahhhh…it's Robin?"

"Oh, great. Just the guy I wanted to talk to," I said, my voice saturated with sarcasm. But way down deep, I found I was really glad to hear his voice.

"You've seen the article. Listen, I didn't write that article, and I didn't know it was going to be in the magazine, and I had nothing to do with it."

"Right."

"I mean, it's good pre-publicity for the movie, but I didn't arrange it."

"Right."

"So, at least, you already know I'm coming back to Lawrenceton?"

"Yes." If I could stick to one syllable at a time, I

might be able to restrain myself. The anger had definitely dominated that little spurt of pleasure.

"The thing is, no matter what the article said about me and Celia, I want to see you again."

To see how I'd aged, how I'd changed? Not for the better, I was sadly aware.

"I heard," Robin said into my silence, "you have a house out in the country now. I hope you'll let me visit you."

"No," I said, and hung up. It didn't really make a difference to which statement I was responding. "No," covered just about everything. Maybe, two years ago, I would have been appalled at my own rudeness. Somehow, marriage and widowhood had given me the indifference to be rude—at least from time to time.

I lay awake in the darkness for a while, thinking over the implications of Robin's call. Was he truly hoping to renew our friendship? I didn't know why; maybe he just wanted me to be fodder for the camera. Or maybe he was just calling because Celia Shaw had told him to call. I didn't like to think of the very young actress leading Robin around by his…nose.

Surely Robin was counting on finding the old Aurora: the one who, in her late twenties, had just discarded her high school wardrobe for something more adult; the one who was just learning to say what she thought; the one who was just on the verge of coming out of her shell. Robin had left town before that process had gotten up a head of steam.

Across the fields, my neighbor Clement Farmer's dog Robert began to bark—at the moon, at a coon, at a wandering cat or derelict dog...who knew? Robert (short for Robert E. Lee) had a barking episode just about every night. I didn't mind, this once; the noise was company for my thoughts.

I found myself wondering how Robin himself had changed. I remembered meeting Robin when he'd moved into the row of townhouses I managed for Mother. I figured that when I'd met Robin, I'd been twenty-nine. Now I'd turned thirty-six. Why, Robin must be forty!

When he first moved to the coast, he'd called me a lot, telling me this and that. His book had gone through three title changes, he'd had trouble getting some of the relatives of the victims and the murderers to talk to him, and one deal had been discarded in favor of another. He'd gone out to California with his agent, and I was pretty sure they'd been more to each other than agent and client but, somewhere along the way, that relationship had changed. His book, finally titled *Whimsical Murder,* had been finished while he was in California.

I'd been angry with him, even then. I'd always hated the idea of a book about the crimes in Lawrenceton. I'd tried to understand his need to write the book, the conviction he'd had that this was the book that would "make" his career. Well, it had. Robin's fiction had all been reprinted in matching paperbacks, *Whimsical Murder* had been on the best-seller list for months, and the paperback was poised to be on the stands the week the movie opened.

My eyes fluttered shut, for just a second of sweet oblivion. My anger against Robin slid off my mind, replaced with a more familiar melancholy.

He'd been living in Hollywood, swimming with the sharks, off and on for the past few years. I would seem even more naïve and provincial to Robin now. I'd had a certain amount of awe for him when we met, because he'd been a fairly well-known mystery writer, teaching a writer-in-residence course at a college in Atlanta. I thought of the day I'd gone into the city to meet him for lunch…I'd worn that ivory blouse with the green ivy pattern…

I could sense sleep approaching now, could feel it stealing over me. I held onto the thought of Robin so I could slide under; if I looked directly at the sleep I needed, it would slip away. Tomorrow I'd check his picture in the magazine again, examine his hair for any signs of gray. I didn't have any yet, but when I spotted some, I'd have Bonita take care of it right away.….

Perry and Lillian were in the library's employee lounge when I got to work, and their conversation ground to a guilty halt when I appeared. Lillian Schmidt beamed at me with her most insincere smile. Believe me, she's got quite a repertoire. Perry Allison just looked nervous, which was about par for the course for Perry. Perry is about half Lillian's age, bone thin and perpetually jumpy, while Lillian is as round and plain as a ball of coarse yarn. Perry, who's been in and out of mental facilities and drug treatment programs, is now on an even keel as long as he takes his medication. Lillian, with whom I have even less in common, is a self-centered member of a fundamentalist Christian church. These are my best work friends. Am I lucky? I stuffed my purse in one of the bright orange lockers while they covered the silence with a spate of chatter that wouldn't have deceived a reasonably intelligent child.

"Good weather for this time of year," Lillian told Perry, who nodded his head in an alarming series of jerks.

"Uh, Roe. We just want you to know we didn't know anything about that writer, or the article, or anything." Perry was trying an ingratiating smile, but it was sliding off the other side of his face. Perry had a difficult life, and he didn't want me mad at him.

"No, hon, we would've told you if we'd known a magazine writer was in the library." Lillian's eyes were bright with excitement.

For all her gusto in the situation, which was the way she was born, I really believed Lillian. For that matter, I believed Perry, who could be quite devious. Other librarians came and went, but we three had been yoked, somewhat off and on for…oh, seven or eight years.

"Okay," I said mildly, but in such a way as to close the subject. They were probably telling the truth, but *someone* had talked to the writer, Marjory Bolton. I thought I could pin the betrayal on the shoulders of the aide who'd been fired last week for stealing from other employees. I was willing to bet she was already out of town and beyond reach. I suggested this to Perry and Lillian, and they jumped on the idea with enthusiasm.

After a second or two of relaxing small talk, both put on their work faces and went through the door to the patron part of the library.

The employee lounge was a large open room with a couple of tables and matching chairs, a small kitchen, and a large worktable in one corner where we repaired books and prepared new ones to be placed on the shelves. Then there was a half-wall with glass in the top, through which you could see Sam Clerrick's secretary's office. Sam's was firmly walled. His secretary wasn't at her desk, but I could see the lights in Sam's office were on. If he wanted to ask me about the article, he'd call me in. Otherwise, I knew he'd appreciate not being disturbed. Sam was a whiz with the budget, could apply for grants with one hand tied behind his back, and he was an absolutely sound administrator.

But Sam was a dismal failure with people. Painfully aware of the fact, he tended to leave all the personnel interactions he possibly could to his secretary, a position he'd manufactured with some creative money managing. Though the job was only part-time, Patricia Bledsoe had made the most of it.

She was coming in the back door now, dressed, as always, in painstakingly matched and ironed clothes. They weren't expensive clothes, but she had good conservative taste and was an ardent shoe polisher. Patricia—not Pat, or Patsy, or Trish—was somewhere around fifty, with skin the color of a Brach's caramel. Her hair was tamed into a short pageboy—not for Patricia the weaves and beads of more trendy African-Americans. Patricia didn't like nail polish, or dark lipstick, or high heels. Her teenager, Jerome, was not allowed to wear clothing sporting a visible brand name: no Nike, no Fubu, and no Reebok. There was a reason behind everything Patricia Bledsoe did, and if she'd ever acted spontaneously, it had been a long time ago in a galaxy far, far, away.

Not too surprisingly, everyone depended on Patricia, but no one liked her very much. The great exception was Sam Clerrick, whom she guarded as though he was a wealthy industrial magnate.

Patricia said, "Good morning, Ms. Teagarden. How are you today?" Her voice was as crisp as if it'd been in the vegetable drawer overnight.

As always, I fought the terrible impulse to imitate her brisk enunciation. "I'm fine, thank you, Patricia. Did you see the magazine with the article about the movie?"

Patricia knew what I was talking about since everyone in Lawrenceton had been buzzing about the movie company's arrival for weeks.

"No, is there something new?" She waited politely for my answer, her beige sweater half-off. Today she was wearing a solid yellow camp shirt with a khaki skirt and yellow espadrilles. It was that kind of weather, cool in the morning and evening but still awfully hot during the day; the kind of Southern weather that makes you think summer will never, ever, be over.

"People don't like to talk about it around me," I said matter-of-factly. "But as far as I could tell, the only thing that isn't common gossip around here is the name of the female lead, and the strange fact that there was someone in the library who was willing to talk to a reporter about me. I hate the idea that someone would do that without talking to me first," I told her.

When her reaction came, it certainly wasn't one I'd been expecting.

Patricia's face tensed. She froze for a beat, and then she finished shrugging off the sweater and sat in her rolling chair in front of her computer.

"That does seem strange," she said, but it seemed to me that she was picking words out of the air at random. The secretary was deeply upset. In fact, she seemed suddenly afraid.

I waited for a second more, but finally I knew that whatever comment Patricia had on news reporters, I wasn't going to hear it.

She did ask me for the name of the magazine. When I told her, she just nodded in thanks and switched on her computer. I'd been dismissed. Her composure was back in place.

Thinking of how perplexing Patricia was, I shrugged and left the staff area to start my working day in my favorite place in the whole world, the library. Any library would have done, but this one was dear to me because the shelves held some of my best friends. While I gathered the books that had come in through the after-hours book drop the night before, I puzzled over Patricia's odd reaction.

It was the first time I'd felt curiosity in months. When I realized how refreshing it felt, I knew that it was good.

Pushing a cart of books through the library, nodding to Mr. Harmon (who came in every morning to read the papers), I had a flood of revelation. (What a time and place to review my life, past and future! But I suddenly realized that when I was alone, my life was the thing I worked hardest to avoid considering.)

As I dislodged one of the cart's rollers from a worn spot in the heavy-duty carpeting, I understood—abruptly and very clearly—that my life had not been bad before I married Martin Bartell. Maybe it hadn't been what I expected, or what anyone would have predicted for me, but it had been livable, with enough surprises and bits of happiness to make it worthwhile and, above all, interesting.

Grief was boring. This was a shallow thought about a deep subject, but it was a valid observation.

When my loss had been fresh, passing every hour had been like hiking through a rocky terrain with a monster hiding behind every other boulder. I'd get my bank statement and remember Martin wasn't there to balance our checkbook anymore. I'd cry. I'd go to the grocery store and remember to get one chicken breast, not two. I'd suffer. There'd be no one in the house to share my day with, no one to take care of. That phase had been jagged, acute, draining, a shock wrapped around every daily occurrence. I missed Martin every day, every hour, sometimes every minute.

But that era had faded, worn thin, and dissipated. Without noting it, I'd entered another phase. The past few months—say, the past six—had been like slogging through a gray swamp. I'd been too exhausted to even open my eyes and look around me. I had routinely forgotten whole conversations, complete transactions, significant events. Nothing had seemed important but my loss.

Right now, just at this split second, I fully comprehended for a fact that my life would go on and there would be things in it I would enjoy.

For the first time, that didn't seem like a betrayal of Martin. Though he'd been the picture of health and his death had been the worst kind of shock, I'd always been aware of the fact that he was fifteen years older than me—that probably, in the natural course of things, I'd have some living to do without him. Events had taken an unnatural course, but the result was the same.

I was getting sniffly, so I concentrated really hard on checking in the books, getting them back to the shelves, returning the cart to its designated spot. Perry and Lillian were always very obviously tactful when my eyes looked red, God bless them, and they were again today.

Two

I looked up Celia Shaw on the Internet that night. My computer was less than two years old, bought by Martin so he could work at home from time to time. I'd learned to use it, at least enough to send and receive email and to search for information. The games bored me, I'd discovered, and my money was "handled" by my accountant, so I only turned the machine on a couple of times a week.

Celia was supposed to be twenty-five, I learned, a figure I took with a grain of salt. She'd been born in Wilmington, North Carolina, where her mother had been working in a movie. I hadn't realized there were movie studios in Wilmington but, according to the article, it was quite a movie-making center. Well, back to Celia. Her mother, Linda Shaw, a middle-aged minor actress, had been so long separated from her husband that the baby's parentage was in doubt. Linda Shaw had left the infant Celia with an aunt and uncle, and fled. Linda resurfaced in California a couple of years later, dead. She'd committed suicide in a motel—barbiturates and a razor combined.

What a tragic beginning.

Though my father had left when I was a teenager, my mother had been a rock. I'd never had aunts and uncles, since both my parents were only children (which may have contributed to their problems), but my mother had a whole network of friends, family connections, and coworkers on whom to call.

Having become more sympathetic to Celia Shaw, whom I'd been quite prepared to dislike, I continued scrolling along. I examined pictures of Celia in various movies I'd never seen. I paused to check out a dress Celia had worn to the Emmy Awards. Hmmm. I was more conservative sartorially than I'd realized.

I peered at the picture. Had she had to glue that bit into place? How had she planned to cope if she'd dropped her purse? Of course, someone would've picked it up for her gladly; Celia Shaw would never have to perform any little service for herself, at least not for the next ten years. Still, what if she'd forgotten her posture and slumped a little....

Well, she had nerve, anyway. I'd give her that.

According to her bio, Celia Shaw had won escalating parts in five minor films and two major television shows. However, *Whimsical Death*, a two-part made-for-TV movie, would constitute her first leading role. Chip Brodnax was taking the role of Robin. His face was familiar to me, but I couldn't remember where I'd seen him. I didn't watch a lot of television, but I was sure I'd noticed him in something before.

The same picture of Celia Shaw that had been in the magazine was on the website, the one of her with Robin at a party. There was another shot of Celia holding her Emmy. She was beautiful, no doubt about it. And even if her given age of twenty-five was literally less than the truth, there was no doubt in my mind that Celia Shaw was several years younger than me.

As I closed down the computer and went upstairs for my bath, I wondered why I'd bothered to search out this information. I told myself it was because she was going to play me—or someone at least as close to me as the movie could go, since I'd refused permission for a character to have my name. Surely it wasn't too surprising that I'd have an interest in the woman who was going to represent me?

I attended Evening Prayer that Wednesday night. This was by no means my normal schedule, I'm sorry to say. St. Stephen's saw me on Sunday mornings, but that was the limit of my church attendance, and I'd dodged the altar guild, the vestry, and the annual Christmas bazaar committee with amazing agility. (I was beginning to have a slightly guilty feeling, as though I watched PBS every night yet didn't send in a dime at pledge time.)

On this balmy evening, I scooted into an empty pew close to the back of the small church and let all my worries go while I moved through the ritual that meant so much to me.

As I was about to shake Father Aubrey Scott's hand while I was going out the door, he said, "Could you stay for a minute? I'd like to have a few words."

"Sure," I said. I'd always been fond of Aubrey. In fact, I'd dated him for many months. Then I'd met Martin and he'd met Emily, and we'd parted amiably. The warmth of a pleasant companionship remained. I rummaged through my mind for any recent hot topics in the congregation that he'd need to discuss with me, but I couldn't come up with a one.

With a sense of mild expectation, I settled on a bench in the quiet churchyard while the other congregants got in their cars and switched on their headlights in the gathering dusk. Soon we'd have the time change. We'd be leaving in the full dark. Through the lighted windows I could see Aubrey's wife, Emily, blond and suburban, moving around the church. She was raising kneelers that had been left down, picking up programs discarded in the pews, and turning out lights. Elizabeth, Emily's daughter by her deceased first husband, hadn't been in church that night. She'd probably used homework to wriggle out of coming; Elizabeth, now ten, was quite a handful. But Aubrey never regretted adopting Elizabeth; he doted on her.

Having divested himself of his robe, Aubrey came to

sit beside me in the half-darkness. Aubrey was a lot grayer than he'd been when he'd first come to Lawrence-ton to take the helm of St. Stephen's. Was Aubrey thirty-nine? Or closer to forty-two? I caught myself frowning: I was thinking about age far too often these days.

"I have something I need to ask you," Aubrey said, sounding very grave.

"Ask ahead," I told him. From the open church door came a *thwack!* as Emily raised the fourth kneeler from the back on the left, which was a little noisier than the others.

"Would it offend you if the movie company filmed some scenes here at the church?" he asked.

Whatever I'd expected, it wasn't this request. I was glad of the darkness, since I had no idea what my face looked like. I couldn't think of what to say.

"The vestry met with the film company representa-tive last night. The thing is," he continued, after a pause to offer me a chance to comment, "they're offering enough in compensation to get a new roof put on St. Stephen's—both the parish hall and the church. But if you have the slightest objection, we'll forego the money. It won't be worth it. You're one of ours. The vote on that was unanimous."

So many comments came to my lips that I com-pressed them together to lock the words inside. There was only one answer I could possibly give. "Of course," I said. "For a new roof, you have to say yes." I knew my voice was much cooler than I wanted it to be, and I knew my words weren't exactly enthusiastic or even very civil, but that was the best I could do.

"You don't sound okay about it," Aubrey said after a hesitation. "You sound like you want me to go play in traffic."

I smiled a little, a very little, but he couldn't see that.

"St. Stephen's is beautiful. I'm not surprised they'd like to use it as a set. Nothing will be changed?"

"He promised not. He said everything would look just the same or better, since the film company will paint the sign on the corner for us."

"Then you'd better do it." It crossed my mind that I could pay for the new church roof, all by myself, and then the film company could go whistle. But that would draw even more attention to me, and that was the one thing I didn't want. I made sure to exchange another comment or two with Aubrey, so he wouldn't think I was leaving angry. He'd given me a choice and I'd picked, so I couldn't take the result of my decision out on him.

By the time Emily locked the door of the church, I was on my way to my car.

Madeleine was waiting at the kitchen door when I got home. Madeleine, golden and fat and increasingly slow, was the living part of the legacy an old friend had left me. Jane had left me the cat and a pot of money. Guess which I liked best? Madeleine was known and feared by every vet in the Lawrenceton area. Fortunately, except for the effects of old age, the cat had always been healthy. Her annual checkups were traumatic for everyone involved. Though I'd grown up without pets, thanks to a mother who thought having animal hair in your house was comparable to having lice, Madeleine and I had coexisted in reasonable harmony for several years now. I fed her, brushed her in the spring and summer, and scratched behind her ears. She ate the food, enjoyed the brushing, purred when I scratched her, and otherwise ignored me. It worked for us.

I watched the huge old cat launch into her kitty chow with gusto. When that palled, I wandered across the hall into the den, admiring the way the wooden floors gleamed and the books marched in even rows in the built-in bookcases in the hall. The answering machine light was blinking by my telephone and for a minute or two I thought about checking my messages.

Then I decided it didn't matter what other people wanted.

Smiling a little, I hiked up the stairs, spent some time in the bathroom on my minimal grooming ritual, and climbed into my high four-poster. I had lots of pillows, a comfortable bed, and a good book.

Martin hadn't really liked my reading in bed. To Martin, a bed was for sleeping in or making love on, not for reading or lolling of any kind. For the most part, I'd read downstairs in the den while we were married. Now, this was one of the moments of the day to which I actually looked forward; and if it was raining outside or cold, or both, and I could swathe myself in blankets, so much the better. The night was mild outside my windows this evening, but as I pulled up the clean sheet I came as close as I could, these days, to being happy. I was reading a new C.J. Songer, too, an added bonus.

Just when I was getting drowsy, the phone rang. I leaned forward to check my caller-ID device. I picked up the phone, already smiling.

Angel said, "I got a question to ask you."

Angel and Shelby Youngblood were both very direct, Angel more so than her husband. Shelby, a Vietnam vet and one of the toughest men I'd ever met, had learned to approach certain topics sideways rather than straight on, something I didn't think would ever occur to Angel. Their little girl Joan was going to have to be one sturdy kid. Already, at nearly a year old, Joan seemed more independent than most babies her age. At least Angel told me so.

"Shoot," I told her.

"You mind if I work this movie? I got a call from a guy who asked if I wanted to do stunts."

Everyone, *everyone*, wanted to work for the damn movie. I had a moment's flash of intense resentment, an irrational conviction that all the people of Lawrenceton should shun the movie and the moviemakers, not rent or sell to them, not be employed by them, and all for my sake, because I didn't want this film made.

"Of course you ought to," I said calmly. "I know it's been years since you got any stunt work, and you must miss it."

"Thanks," Angel said. She was so direct herself that it seldom occurred to her that people didn't exactly mean what they said. "If you're sure. We're trying to save up for a swimming pool for Joan."

"Above ground?"

"Nope, in-ground. So we got a ways to go."

I silently exhaled. "Well, you better get to it. Bye, Angel."

"See you soon, Roe."

I thought it was the perfect cap to a perfect day. *What could happen tomorrow,* I asked myself rhetorically, *that would make it any worse than today?*

I should have known better than to ask myself any such a thing.

Three

I didn't have to work that Thursday, so I didn't get up until about seven-thirty. Catherine Quick, the maid, was supposed to be coming in that afternoon, so I didn't have to make my bed; she'd be changing the sheets. I trotted down the stairs to put on the coffeepot, and I popped an English muffin in the toaster before I went to the living room at the front of the house to look out. Though the air was chilly that morning, making me glad I'd pulled on jeans and a sweater before I came downstairs, it was going to warm up and be a beautiful day. The air was crystal clear, the sky so blue it almost sparkled. I told myself I wouldn't worry that day, wouldn't think about the movie at all. Maybe I would call Sally Allison to see if she could have lunch with me. Since she was a reporter, Sally always knew what was going on in Lawrenceton.

The kitchen had two doors, the back one opening onto our patio, and the side one opening under the covered walkway leading to the garage. Madeleine's cat flap was in the patio door, and she made an entrance just about this time every morning, tired from her night's adventures and ready to eat her kibble. But this morning, though I filled her bowl and renewed her water, she didn't show. Maybe I'd see her when I went down the long driveway to fetch my newspaper.

I opened the side door and made a noise somewhere between a gasp and a shriek. The young man sitting on the steps jumped up, dumping Madeleine off his lap in the process.

"Hello, Aurora," he said, and in that moment I recognized him.

"Hello, Barrett," I said, trying hard not to sound as anxious and angry as I felt. It was all I could do not to blurt out, "What do you want?" At six feet, Barrett was tall enough to cow me, and of course he was fit, since looking good was part of his stock in trade. His hair was a new color, a dark blond, and he was wearing glasses he didn't need.

It's an accurate measure of our relationship that I wondered, just in a flash, if Barrett had come disguised so no one would recognize him in the police lineup after my body was discovered.

"I didn't know you were in Lawrenceton," I said, my voice much more shaky than I liked.

"Oh, yes. And I came to see you first thing, Stepmom."

So it was going to be that way.

As if it had ever been any other way.

"Barrett, what are you doing here?" I was not stable enough emotionally to put up with all this parrying.

"Just wanted to come check in on you, see how you were enjoying my dad's money," he said casually. The actor. I wondered how often he'd rehearsed tossing that line over to me.

I sighed. I considered several responses, most based on my new policy of rudeness, but a sudden deep exhaustion quenched anything I might have said.

"Frankly, Barrett, I don't enjoy much of anything." My voice was as weary as I felt. It was time to speak plainly, and end this if it was possible. I stepped back and said, "Come in, if you have to, and say whatever you have to say. I'm sorry we misunderstood each other so badly after your father died. I just wasn't at my most intelligent or sensitive."

Barrett's face was already arranged to say something witty and cruel. But there was a subtle shift in his expression as he listened. He nearly relented, but at the last second his grievance settled back on his shoulders like a cape. "Did your lawyer tell you to say that?" he sneered.

I could think of no response. "Do you want some coffee? Have you had breakfast yet?" When in doubt, fall back on being a lady, as my mother had always advised me—though truly, it would feel better to kick Barrett in the butt.

Once again, Mother was proved right. Barrett had no idea how to pose himself. "I'd like a cup of coffee," he said after an appreciable pause. "I take it black." He looked around the kitchen with almost palpable surprise. What had he expected—marble countertops and a resident chef? It was just an ordinary kitchen. I got another cup from the cabinet and buttered my English muffin, which had popped up.

"So, what are you doing here in Lawrenceton?" I asked. "I guess you came to visit your dad's grave? I got the headstone in about four months ago. It looks real nice." I took a deep breath, trying unsuccessfully to repress the tears that welled up. I grabbed a tissue and blotted my eyes. I glanced over at my stepson as I put his coffee on the table, to surprise a look of shame on his face.

"You didn't even think of going out to the cemetery," I said out loud. I was truly stunned.

"He's not really there," Barrett said, scrambling for a defense. He sat down at the table and looked sullen.

"No, of course not," I said numbly. I put half my muffin in front of Barrett. "And I know I shouldn't have spent so much time out there at first, but somehow you just want to be close…I know that's stupid." I shook my head. I could feel the trembles and weepies looming, like unpleasant relatives due for a visit.

Barrett was staring at me like he'd never seen me before. He took a sip of his coffee. "You've lost weight," he said at last.

I shrugged. "Maybe a little." It was my turn to drink some coffee. My eyes ached with tears. But this, too, would pass. "I suppose your check got to you all right?" Martin's will had finally been probated; of course, money was at the root of Barrett's rancor.

"Yes," he said.

The silence dragged uncomfortably. "I'm sorry, again, about the—about the misunderstanding after Martin died."

"No," said Barrett sharply. "Let's not talk about that."

Which was fine with me. In the turmoil after Martin's death, I had simply forgotten that Martin's adult son had been in the habit of receiving handouts from Martin when acting jobs proved few and far between. For one thing, the largesse had been irregular; Martin had always thought it would be an insult to give Barrett a steady allowance, as though Barrett were still a child. So he waited until Barrett called and hinted that he needed a "loan," and then Martin would mail a check. Once I'd become aware of this practice, I'd bitten my tongue to prevent myself commenting.

Most importantly, it was none of my business. I had my own money, and Martin's checks to Barrett had not deprived me of anything at all. But in my opinion, if Martin thought it right to support an adult son, he should have made it a regular arrangement, so Barrett wouldn't have to ask.

My lips were sealed even more tightly because Barrett loathed me and always had. He'd dodged coming to our wedding, at family functions he never addressed me directly if he could avoid it, he'd only visited Lawrenceton when I was out of town, and he'd made it insultingly clear (out of his dad's hearing) that he thought I was marrying Martin for his money.

So in the months immediately after my husband's funeral, Barrett's financial state had been the last thing on my mind. But one night Barrett had called me, when he'd held out as long as he could for his legacy. Probate often takes much longer than it has any right to, and in the case of Martin's estate, which was a little complicated because of his diverse holdings—real estate, stock, insurance payments, and the retirement fund of Pan-Am Agra—well, settling Martin's affairs was a drawn-out process. That night, Barrett had stiffly demanded I mail him the money he was accustomed to getting.

I hadn't reacted well. I could tell how difficult it was for Barrett to call, but in my view, he should have been man enough to manage on his own rather than phone me. At the same time, I admit I was aware that Barrett must truly have his back to the wall financially to be driven to such a measure. But I was just too mired in my personal hell to care about Barrett's problems. He could have helped me in many ways when Martin had died—just being civil would have been a good way to start—and he had chosen not to do so. Now, I chose not to help him. I'd told him so, frankly and at length, being unable to think beyond the moment and see this from any other angle than the one in front of my face.

The next day I'd woken up sorry, but not because I hadn't solved Barrett's financial problems. I'd been sorry because Martin had loved Barrett, and would have wanted me to send the money—no matter what it said about Barrett that he'd even asked me for it. So without calling or writing a note to enclose, I'd FedExed Barrett a check—my own money—for what he'd needed.

I'd never heard a word from him after that, until this moment. I'd sent him his share of Martin's estate when it had all been settled. I had not deducted what I'd already given him. That would have been businesslike, but he would have taken it as petty. I just didn't want to struggle with Barrett any more.

So here we were, not talking about the incident that lay between us, as big and smelly as a dead fish.

I cleared my throat and asked after his mother and aunt. Cindy's florist shop was doing well, Barrett said. In fact, Cindy and her partner were expanding the shop to include gifts and home-decorating items. "They took out a loan," Barrett made a point of telling me, I guess so I'd realize he couldn't have turned to his mother for money. "She and Dennis plan to get married."

"I'm glad for them," I said, not caring one little bit.

"Aunt Barby has been keeping Regina's baby for a week or two, while Regina and her husband are on vacation in New York."

While I was indifferent about Cindy, I actively disliked Martin's sister Barby and her daughter Regina, who was on her second marriage. I was confident that

Regina would someday be on her fourth. Probably she would have had a few more babies along the way.

"Why didn't you and Dad have any children?" Barrett asked me. The question came from out of the blue and lodged in my heart.

"I can't have children," I said. "We talked about it a little, before we found out that I had some fertility problems. I sure wanted a baby, and sometimes he did too. But he was a little wary of starting a new family at his age." I saw Martin, so clearly, leaning over Regina's baby when I'd placed him beside Martin on our bed. Tears trickled down my cheeks. I lowered my face and wiped it with a napkin. "Can I get you some more coffee?" I asked politely.

"No, thank you. I need to be getting back." Barrett and I both stood up. He scrabbled through his pockets for the car keys, and looked uncertain, not a normal Barrett state of mind.

He looked as though he were going to make some kind of pronouncement, but in the end, all he said was, "Thanks for the coffee." It wasn't until I watched his car turn onto the county road that I realized he'd never told me why he was in Lawrenceton.

It didn't take long for the other shoe to drop. While I was upstairs covering up the circles under my eyes and brushing my hair, it suddenly occurred to me that Barrett was in town because he had a part in the movie. I couldn't imagine why I hadn't made the connection earlier. He would be a natural choice for the cast, as the stepson of one of the real-life figures in our local drama. He'd even visited Lawrenceton before, when I'd been gone with my mother to a real estate convention in Orlando.

I collapsed ungracefully on the delicate peach-colored chair in the corner of the bedroom and further considered this likelihood. Barrett was an up-and-coming actor, whose longest running part had been on a popular soap. I think he played a seductive chauffeur. Since I never watch daytime television, I'd never seen him in it—which, now that I came to examine my conduct, was just as much stubbornness as his refusing to come to our wedding—but several women who knew of our connection had told me how good he was. They'd had their tongues hanging out as they said it, too.

I wondered what role Barrett would have. I wondered, for the first time, what the script was like; how close the movie would come to the reality.

I wished I hadn't hung up on Robin Crusoe.

Moved by an impulse I didn't even want to analyze, I decided to go shopping that morning. My friend Amina Day's mother owned a women's clothing store called Great Day. If I bought anything in Lawrenceton, rather than going to my favorite store in Atlanta, I bought it at Great Day. To my pleasure, Mrs. Day had a younger partner now, and the selection had really improved as a result.

I had a closet full of good clothes already, but I

needed something new, some voice deep within me advised. My coloring—brown hair, brown eyes, fair complexion—was pretty neutral, so my color field was wide open. As Barrett had noticed, I'd lost weight I'd never regained when Martin died, so my involuntarily smaller size was another excuse for shopping.

As I got out of my car at the strip mall that housed Great Day, a cluster of people emerged from the Crafts Consortium next door. Homemade quilts, candles, and all kinds of "country" stuff formed the bulk of the store's goods, and crowds were not something I'd ever seen there. The center of the group seemed to be a short, thin, very young woman with artistically disheveled blond hair who was wearing the highest heels I'd ever seen on a woman who wasn't standing on a street corner. And these high heels were worn with jeans, the tightest jeans I'd ever seen. No, wait; Nadine Gortner had worn some just as tight to one of the Pan-Am Agra picnics, and her zipper had popped.

As if the heels and jeans weren't enough to mark her out, this woman had lips outlined in the darkest possible shade of red while the lipstick she'd filled in with was a creamy pink. She looked like a bee had been at her.

The people accompanying this creature were not as eye-popping, which was a relief. An older, grizzled man who might be from almost anywhere was carrying a bag (which I had to believe belonged to The Creature). A slightly less ornate woman in a modified version of The Creature's outfit was scrabbling in her outsize purse with fingernails like a Chinese emperor's. She pulled out some car keys, and immediately reached out to steady her flamboyant friend, who had stumbled on the irregular surface of the parking lot. No wonder, in those heels.

After absorbing this trio in a comprehensive glance, I passed them with my eyes straight forward. That was why I noticed Miss Joe Nell standing in the glass door of Great Day making an elaborate face at me, jabbing her finger vehemently in the direction of the little group. It was hard to keep a steady course forward, since Amina's mom was doing her best to get me to stop, turn, and stare.

"That was them!" she said excitedly, as soon as I came through the door. Miss Joe Nell and her partner, Mignon Derby, were flushed and practically panting.

"Them?" I said, trying not to sound as irritated as I felt.

"The movie people!" Without ever thinking that I might not be delighted to have come in close proximity with some "movie people," the two women began speaking all at once. Miss Joe Nell and Mignon (who, at twenty-eight, had the kind of skin most women only dream of) were extremely revved up about the trio's just-concluded visit to Great Day, where the Starlet Lite (as opposed to the spike-heeled Full Starlet) had bought a white linen shell.

"I don't know what Celia Shaw bought at Crafts Consortium," Mignon babbled. "I'm gonna go call Teal and find out!"

So that had been Robin's girlfriend, at least according to the magazine article. I was almost proud for despising her before I had known. Then I was angry with myself for my lack of charity. This was not my day to be pleased with the way I conducted my life.

I am not exactly poker-faced, so Miss Joe Nell was picking up on my lack of enthusiasm.

"Well, that was fun, but we know who's going to be around when the movie people are gone," she said, smiling. "What can I show you today, Roe?"

Since I didn't know what I wanted, I felt even grumpier. I was rapidly getting to be the town killjoy. At that moment, I was sure I was the only person in Sparling County who wished everyone associated with the movie project would fall into a big hole.

I calmed down as I shopped, the familiar ritual and the renewed attentiveness of Mignon and Miss Joe Nell combining to make me feel once again that I had a legitimate place in the world.

Hmmm. Was I just full of sour grapes at not being Top Dog? Was I way too used to having people treat me with a little deference and a little extra attention because I was well-heeled and a widow?

Just could be.

A life unexamined is not a life lived, I reminded myself, and resolved to be a little less stuffy and a lot less grudging about the excitement the filmmaking was bringing to Lawrenceton. Maybe, despite my legitimate gripes about the movie's being made at all, what I was really doing was…pouting. Hmmm, indeed.

I left with a nice bulky bag and lots of news about Amina, since Miss Joe Nell and her husband were just back from a trip to Dallas to see Hugh, Amina, and their two-year-old, Megan, who was being taught to call me Aunt Roe.

Spending money always makes me feel better, so I drove to my lunch engagement with Sally Allison with a lighter heart. Sally was waiting in the foyer of the restaurant, wearing her usual solid colors—today she sported a bronze silk blouse under a tan pants suit— and groping in her huge shoulder bag. She pulled out a phone and dialed while I watched. Holding up a finger to let me know she'd just be a minute, Sally told her adult son Perry to be sure to take his clothes by the cleaners that day. I raised my eyebrows, and Sally had the self-awareness to look a little embarrassed.

"Once a mother, always a mother," she said after she'd hung up.

"Let's get in line, unless you want to call someone else?"

"No, I'll turn it off during lunch," she said bravely, and pressed a button. "When are you going to join the twenty-first century?"

"I have a cell phone. I just don't turn it on unless I want to call someone."

"But…but…it's to use!"

"Not if I don't want to," I said.

Sally clearly loved her cell phone and, since she was a reporter, I could see that it would be a valuable tool for her. But to me, it was just a nuisance. I got too many phone calls as it was, without arranging for a way to get more.

Sally told me all about Perry's new girlfriend as we moved down the line. I got my tray from the stack, and my silverware, and ordered ice tea and beef tips over rice. I got my number and looked for a free table while Sally ordered. Beef 'N More seemed quite crowded, and I wondered a little at that—but it was a popular place, especially with the noon business crowd.

"See, these are movie people," Sally hissed as she unloaded her tray and put her receipt faceup where the waitress could spot it when she brought our food. "Isn't this something?"

Even Sally, the toughest woman I knew, was dizzy with excitement about the damn movie. I remembered my good resolutions, and I managed not to look sour.

"Where are they all staying?"

"The Ramada out by the interstate, most of them," Sally said after she put down her little packet of sweetener and stirred the powder vigorously into her tea. "That Celia Shaw has the Honeymoon Suite. But the director—Joel Park Brooks—is renting Pinky Zelman's house. I hope Pinky's asking a lot of money, because I bet it won't be in any great shape when he moves out." Sally looked a little pleased, as if the prospect of writing a story about the director's damage to Dr. Pincus Zelman's house was a treat Sally had in store.

Clearly, Sally was seeing stories, stories just lining up

to be written. What a bonanza this was going to be for the *Sentinel*.

"Are you going to watch them filming?" I asked.

"Every chance I get. And they've hired me as a consultant." Sally flushed with pride.

"That makes sense. You did the best series of stories on the murders, after all." Those stories had nearly bumped Sally up to a bigger paper in a bigger city, but somehow it just hadn't happened. Now, Sally was in her late forties, and she no longer expected that someday she'd leave Lawrenceton, as far as I could tell.

"Thanks, Roe." Sally looked pensive for a moment, her square, handsome face crumpling around the eyes and mouth. "At least," she said, less cheerfully, "now I can finally finish paying all Perry's hospital bills."

"That's great." For the last few years, Perry had been doing very well, but I knew the bills for his treatment had been staggering. Sally had been whittling away at this debt. "Can we have a bill-burning, or some kind of celebration?"

"I'd love it, but it would make Perry feel bad," she said regretfully. "He hates to be reminded of the cost of all that help I gave him. As if I grudged it. It was worth every penny."

"Did Perry pay for any of it?" I regretted the question as soon as it left my lips.

"No, it was my bill, and I paid it," Sally said, after a moment's hesitation. "And don't you say one word about it, Aurora. Perry's a young man; he doesn't need any burdens. He needed to put all his resources into the effort of getting well and staying well. And getting married!"

I clamped my mouth shut. After a moment, I asked Sally how her chef salad was.

And that was the way it went the rest of the meal. We stayed superficial.

In addition to Catherine's old car, there was a black Taurus parked in my driveway. The rental company must specialize in Tauruses. Tauri? Sitting on its gleaming hood was Robin Crusoe.

I got out of my car slowly, uncertain about how I felt about seeing Robin again after all these years. I'd forgotten how tall he was, at least six three. And he'd filled out quite a bit. I remembered Robin as being weedy thin when he'd lived in my mother's townhouse. His hair was as bright a red, and his mouth as quirky, and his nose was the same sharp beak. He was wearing dark glasses, which he whipped off and stuck in his pocket as I approached. He stood—and stood, and stood. I put the Great Day bag on the ground, and kept walking toward him, and he held out his arms. I walked right into them. I wrapped my own around him.

Robin said, "I didn't know if you'd throw something at me or not."

"It was a toss-up," I admitted. I leaned back to look up at his face. "I've been brooding and pouting."

He smiled down at me, and I smiled back. It was hard to resist smiling at Robin.

"How was L.A.?" I asked.

Robin's mobile face darkened and all of a sudden he seemed ten years older. "Unbelievable," he said. "I learned a lot. The thing is, I didn't want to know most of what I learned."

"You'll have to tell me all about it." I recalled his changed circumstances, his relationship with Celia Shaw. "If you have any free time, that is." I released him and stepped back.

"Will you show me your house?"

"Yes." I unlocked the door and punched in the security code. I half-expected Robin to say something about the security system, but he must have gotten accustomed to them while he lived on the West Coast.

"Catherine!" I called. "I'm here with a friend."

"Hey, Roe," she called from upstairs. "I'm just about done."

Robin looked at the bright kitchen, done in cream with orange touches, and went into the hall, admiring the built-in bookcases and the hardwood floors. The den, which was warm in dark blue and deep red, drew a compliment, and the dining room and living room got a nod. There was one smallish bedroom downstairs, and he glanced in its door.

"What's upstairs?" he asked.

"Two bedrooms and a small room Martin kept his workout stuff in," I said.

"I'm sorry, Roe," Robin said.

I kept my gaze averted. "Thanks," I said briefly.

"Would you like to see the patio? We added it on after we moved in, and I wonder sometimes if it wasn't a mistake."

As I was about to open the kitchen door, the cat flap vibrated and Madeleine wriggled through. "I've never seen that fat a cat," Robin said, clearly impressed. "Is this Madeleine?"

"The one and only." I'd inherited Madeleine after Robin left Lawrenceton, but I remembered writing him about the big orange cat.

The patio forgotten, Robin bent to hold out his hand to Madeline. She glared at him after she sniffed it. Pointedly, she turned her back to him and waddled off to her food bowl. It was empty, and she sat in front of it with the air of someone who could wait all day. She would, too. I got out her kibble and filled her bowl. When food was in front of her Madeleine ignored the rest of the world, and she dove in as eagerly as usual.

Catherine came downstairs, her feet heavy on the treads. Catherine was the most consistent "help" I'd ever had. Mostly women came to work for me, showed up on time at first, and then drifted on to some other job. Sometimes they'd tell me; sometimes they just wouldn't show up. Cleaning houses is not for everyone. It's not high-paying, at least in Lawrenceton, and some people seem to feel it's degrading. So I was grateful for Catherine's consistency, and I tried hard to be a good employer.

"I'm fixing to leave," she said, after I'd introduced her to Robin. "You need to get some more Clorox and some more Bounce sheets. I put it on the list on the refrigerator."

"Thanks, Catherine," I said.

"See you next time."

"Okay."

We were never going to be best friends, but at least our exchanges were always civil. After she'd left, I poured some iced tea for Robin and we went into the study, den, downstairs room—I'd called it all three. There was a red leather couch with its back to the window. Robin settled on that, so he'd have plenty of room for his long legs. I had a low, comfortable armchair that allowed my feet to sit firmly on the floor. We looked at each other a little anxiously, not knowing what to say next.

"Are you very unhappy about the movie?" he asked abruptly.

"I was. I'm still not exactly thrilled." I took a deep breath, exhaled. I was making an effort to be honest, with a little tact thrown in. "But the town is very excited, and the money will be good for its economy."

Robin nodded, and seemed to want to change the subject. He started playing "How is?" and we went down a list of names rapidly. It was an unpleasant surprise to me to find how long it had been since I'd seen some of the people Robin asked about. There seemed no excuse for it in a town the size of Lawrenceton.

"Tell me about your husband," Robin said out of the blue.

I sat and stared at my hands for a minute. "Martin was…a senior executive at Pan-Am Agra," I said carefully. "He was older than me by almost fifteen years. He was a Vietnam vet. He was very…dynamic. He had done some shady things in his life. He was always looking for that to come back at him." He loved me deeply. He was fantastic in bed. He was extremely competitive with other men. He was domineering even when he didn't think he was being so. He really listened to me. He broke my heart. I loved him very much, though our marriage had loose edges and rough patches. All this.

"I know you must have some hard times," Robin said quietly. "My mother lost my dad earlier this year, and she's been struggling."

I nodded. Hard times, indeed. "I'm sorry about your dad," I told him, and for a minute we sat in silence.

"Are you going to marry the actress?" I asked brightly, trying to get us back on a less dangerous track. "I saw you-all's picture in the magazine."

"You can't believe the stories about me and Celia," he said. "At one time they had some truth to them, but not any more. We're just barely friends, now."

I raised my eyebrows at him, making a skeptical face.

He grinned. "No, really. She's full of ambition, she's really young, and she's got different priorities. Since she won the Emmy, in fact…well, the only reason she's doing this project is because she'd signed on for it prior to her win." He looked like a different man when he said this, older and harder.

I gave his disenchantment a moment of respectful silence. Then I asked, "So, what did you want from this visit to me?" He must want something, I was sure.

He paid me the compliment of not protesting he'd just wanted to see me again. "I want you to come to the set, at least once. I want you to see this being filmed, read the script."

"Why? Why on earth would you want that?"

"Because I want you...to approve. At least, not to hate it so much."

"Does it really matter to you?"

"Yes." Robin was dead serious.

For the life of me, I couldn't figure out why my approval made any difference at all. But what did I have to lose? I wasn't scheduled to work tomorrow until late afternoon.

"Okay, Robin. I'll come tomorrow to observe for a little while."

"Great," he said, brightening. "I'll set it up."

Four

You would've thought the circus had come to town.

It was the biggest mess I'd ever seen, but I was pretty sure that was because I didn't understand what was happening. There were people everywhere, standing in clusters talking seriously or buzzing busily around the area that had been delineated with sawhorses. A sizeable number of the cast and crew found time to stop by a table laden with bagels and fruit and coffee, a table supervised by a stout, auburn-haired young woman in a white uniform with "Molly's Moveable Feasts" embroidered on the chest.

It appeared that Robin himself was barely tolerated on the set, which surprised me. No one seemed pleased to see him or gave him more than a nod. Writing fame was no guarantee of special treatment here.

"How come they're not happy to have you on the spot?" I asked.

"Writers are just a pain on the set," he explained. He didn't seem at all ruffled or surprised by the indifference shown him. I couldn't believe that Robin was being herded into a corner and practically treated as if he were invisible. To me, writers were the most important people around. I noticed that I was invisible by extension, and that was fine with me.

I only dared talk to Robin in whispers. I tried to figure out what I was seeing, and after a while I asked him to interpret the scene for me.

"That's the director," he said in a low voice, nodding toward a tall, gawky man with five earrings on one ear, a shaved head, and an irritating black goatee. He was wearing an absolutely conventional oxford-cloth shirt and khakis, not only clean and pressed, but also starched. Somehow, with the shaved head and goatee, the shirt and khakis looked odder than a Limp Bizkit tee shirt and cutoffs would have. "His name is Joel Park Brooks, and he's smart as hell. That's his assistant, Mark Chesney, to his right." Mark Chesney was as sunny as Joel Park Brooks was grim, and he was wearing exactly the same kind of clothes. It just didn't look like a costume on Mark Chesney.

"Who's that?" I indicated the graying, rough-looking man I'd seen with Starlets One and Two yesterday.

"That's the head cameraman, Will Weir. He's worked everywhere," Robin said admiringly. "He's easy to work with, they say, and very good."

"Is that Celia?" Starlet One had come out of a trailer

and was striding toward the churchyard. She was recognizable only by her walk, as far as I was concerned. Her hair was tame, her makeup looked very moderate, her clothes were definitely more modest than yesterday's outfit. As I watched, she stumbled on something on the sidewalk, and righted herself with a little jerk. Joel Park Brooks didn't seem to notice, but the cameraman—Will Weir, I reminded myself—frowned as he observed the misstep.

"Yes," Robin said, and he didn't sound glad, or unhappy—any reaction I would have expected from someone seeing the woman he'd dated until fairly recently. He sounded...worried, concerned. Odd. After all, anyone can stumble. I am no graceful swan myself.

Celia hadn't closed the door to her trailer, which was a sort of queenlike omission. I saw the wind blow in and ruffle the pile of papers on the floor, so I stepped closer to take care of the door; and, also, just to satisfy my curiosity. I saw a couch inside the tiny room, a little table sitting by that, and on top of a pile of what seemed to be a manuscript and some library books was an Emmy...the real, bonafide statue. I wondered if Celia would let me hold it, because surely I'd never in my life set eyes on one again. But Robin was looking at me strangely, so I swung the door closed.

Robin pointed out the producer, a wild-haired burly man dressed all in black. "Jessie Bruckner. He's going to be catching an afternoon plane back to L.A.," Robin told me. I had heard of Jessie Bruckner, so I was properly impressed. People seemed to be moving around more purposefully now, and Joel Park Brooks was shouting directions at top speed, so apparently something was about to happen. I was so engrossed in the scene around me that I didn't register my stepson's presence for a while, but then I noticed him waiting by the door of the church, dressed in a conservative suit and tie. He was wearing faux glasses and carrying a Bible. In character, I assumed.

"Who's Barrett playing?"

"Bankston." Robin looked down at me to see if I thought that was funny, and I managed a smile. Of course, the real Bankston Waites had never worn glasses, or carried a Bible, as far as I could remember. He had gone to church, but not this one. Oh well, I guessed accuracy mattered only so much.

Fleetingly, I thought of how much Martin would have relished his son working in Lawrenceton. Then I thought of how happy it would make me if I never had to speak to Barrett again.

When I turned my attention back to what was happening around me, I could see that the actual area the cameras were trained on held no one but actors. Everyone seemed to be at his or her workstation. An amazing amount of food had vanished from the service table, and the stout young woman in white was cleaning away the remnants. She smiled and waved at Robin as he glanced her way.

Silence reigned. As two well-dressed extras took their

places on the sidewalk facing away from the church door, I glanced up at Robin to see him absorbed in the scene before me. He draped a long arm around my shoulders as if that were automatic. I stood stiff and frozen, my own arms crossed across my ribs, trying not to be ridiculously self-conscious about a casual gesture.

At the director's signal, the scene began. It appeared this was supposed to be a Sunday morning, right after church was over. A silver-haired man in priest's robes was standing to the right of the open door, shaking hands as "parishioners" came out. So warm and caring did he look, so saintly was his bearing, that he practically reeked of goodness. The couple already in the churchyard stepped briskly past the cameras. One or two other people came down the church steps. Then one of the "churchgoers" swatted at a wasp, and Joel Park Brooks called the action to a halt.

"Again, without the swatting!" he called, and the actors obediently went back into the church. The couple resumed their place on the sidewalk. The priest's aura of Godliness wavered and then snapped back into place as the action began again.

This time, Celia Shaw (the "me" composite) and Chip Brodnax (I gathered he was the Robin character) made it out of the church. They were positioned in the foreground, while the church emptied behind them.

"I hope you enjoy your stay in our little town," Celia told Chip. Her accent was generically southern. I rolled my eyes, all to myself. Why can't Hollywood comprehend that there are regional accents in the south, besides Cajun? "Lawrenceton's always been so quiet, so safe," she drawled.

"This is a fantastic town," Chip said enthusiastically, staring down at Celia with transparent admiration. "And I know I'm gonna love living here. What do you do for excitement?"

"Why don't you come to a meeting of our club tonight?" Celia said, smiling with delight at her own inspiration. Then she added naughtily, "I'm the guest speaker tonight, and you'd better bone up on…murder!" Then she marched off, head triumphantly in the air, as Chip stared after her, cute bafflement written across his handsome features.

"Cut!" cried a hoarse male voice, and immediately Joel Park Brooks launched himself toward the waiting Chip and Celia.

"You wrote that?" I asked, trying not to sound too horrified.

"No. They hired a script doctor after I turned my version in." Robin's cheeks were red with embarrassment. Or maybe it was just the heat.

The day was definitely getting warm. In October, our night temperatures drop down into the forties pretty often, but the day temperatures can march right back up into the eighties. People were discarding jackets all over the set. I was wearing a short-sleeved dark blue silk tee shirt and khakis, having decided to be cold for an hour rather than tote a sweater the rest of the day. I felt smug. Robin was equally practical in jeans and green golfing shirt. The jeans made his butt look very nice.

"Interested?" Robin asked, and for an unnerving moment I misunderstood him. I looked up at him with wide eyes until I realized he was just asking if I was enjoying the controlled chaos around me. I nodded. Looking past Robin's shoulder, I saw someone waving in his direction. "Hey, that gal wants to talk to you," I said. It was the stout young woman who'd been overseeing the Molly's Moveable Feasts table.

Robin looked uncomfortable. "What now?" he said, and strode off. I was left standing in the middle of a sea of busy people and mysterious cables. I was afraid to move for fear I'd go where I wasn't supposed to, or trip over something vital. It was hard to look nonchalant, under the circumstances, and I was relieved when the chief cameraman stopped to chat.

Though he might be on the unpolished side—his hair was rough and poorly cut, his face almost obscured by a huge graying mustache—he was really polite. "Will Weir," he said, extending a hand. I shook it and introduced myself.

"Oh, yeah, Robin said he was bringing you to the set," Weir said. "Celia's character is based on you, you know."

"I'd heard," I said dryly.

"Robin is a nice guy," Weir said. "I don't know how much of the script is autobiographical, but according to the book, you two dated for a while?"

It seemed a strange thing for this cameraman to ask.

Why would he care? Our relationship was really none of his business. But there wasn't any reason for me to be touchy, either.

"We dated for a couple of months," I said levelly. "Then he went off to Los Angeles to seek his fame and fortune."

Weir appeared to relax at that, and I wondered if he'd been worried that Robin would be distracted by me and thus upset the star of the movie.

Celia seemed upset by something, anyway. Weir heard her voice just as I did, raised in a sharp protest over something. The actress was just far enough away, in a little huddle with the director and Chip Brodnax, to be unintelligible from where we stood. But there was no mistaking the anger in her posture. Her right hand swung out almost as if she intended to slap the much taller director, but Joel Park Brooks proved quick on his feet. He dodged the swinging hand adroitly, and stared down at the actress with a stony face.

Celia herself seemed appalled at what she'd done. For a long moment she looked from Joel to Chip to her own hand, her mouth open in amazement. Then, her body language unmistakable, she apologized.

All three lowered their voices and bent their heads together, and then Joel was striding back to his chair, his shaved head shining in the sun. He'd have to put on a hat soon, or he'd be sorry tomorrow.

Chip and Celia moved back into their starting positions for the scene, as did the first couple, and then…everyone did the whole thing over again.

By the fifth time, Robin was back by my side, with a murmured apology that I didn't quite catch. I was bored, hot, and ready to leave, and I was none too happy with being dumped and reloaded by Robin so unceremoniously. As I whispered my own deliberately unintelligible farewell, my nose was probably as high in the air as Celia's when she did her "pert" sentence.

"I'll call you," he promised. He still seemed distracted. "I think tomorrow we're doing street scenes."

Well, the heck with him, I thought, making my path through the confusing tangle of cables and equipment. I was determined to reach my car and make my getaway. Just as I cleared the edges of the scene and stepped through the tape that held back onlookers, I heard a breathless voice call my name.

"Miss Teagarden!" The caller had a husky, sexy voice, and I turned to find Starlet Two hurrying after me.

"Yes?" I tried to sound more civil than I felt.

"Please, Miss Teagarden, I'm Meredith Askew." She waited a moment, hoping I'd recognize the name. She gave a resigned little sigh when I didn't. "Celia was hoping you could eat dinner with her tonight?" As though this were a great favor.

I bit back my first response, which was, "For God's sake, why?" "No, thanks," I told the girl. It sounded lumpishly ungracious, even to me.

"Oh, but..." Meredith Askew looked disconcerted and unhappy. I looked up at her with more attention.

I'd believe this one was twenty-six, or twenty-one, for that matter. "Celia really wants to talk to you."

"What about?"

"Well, about the script, I guess."

"I don't know anything about the script," I observed.

"She'd like to know what you felt when your mother opened the chocolate box and almost ate one. And it was poisoned."

"What do you think I felt?" I asked incredulously.

"Oh, please come," Meredith said pleadingly.

She was an actress herself, so I should've known better. This not-too-subtle show of terrified innocence, intended to convey that the seasoned and ruthless older actress would torture Meredith if she didn't produce me, couldn't be real. But, I admit, I was beginning to wonder what all this was really about. Besides, what else did I have on my schedule, besides another evening at home with Madeleine?

"All right," I said, sounding as grumpy as I surely was. "Where?"

"We made reservations in Atlanta at Heavenly Barbecue," Meredith said, relaxing openly. "We heard that was the best place to get a taste of the South." I had to keep reminding myself that she was an actress, and that relaxing openly would be the reaction she selected, not necessarily her true feeling. "You can drive over there with us in one of the Range Rovers. We'll leave at eight."

That seemed mighty late to eat, but I nodded shortly and agreed to meet them at the Ramada right off the interstate, where most of the cast and crew were staying. "Though Joel's renting his own house," Meredith said, trying not to sound too envious.

I'd turned to leave when a sudden thought rambled through my head. "Meredith," I called. The young woman turned to look at me, forcing her features into Concerned. "Will Barrett be coming?" I asked. She scanned my face to pick the answer I wanted.

"No," Meredith said, finally. I was quite unsure if she were telling the truth or lying. Lying, I thought, and sighed as I thought of an evening of awkwardness. I'd accepted, though, and I would keep my word. Meredith turned away to go back to her business, whatever it was, and I plotted my route back to my car.

With some difficulty, I picked my way among the cables, trailers, and people. The fringe of the set was becoming heavily populated with Lawrencetonians who had nothing better to do, and I had to stop to meet and greet five or six people who had a thousand questions.

After staggering along the street for two blocks, I had to admit I'd lost my car. I pressed the Open button on my keypad, which would make the lights blink. I looked from side to side. Nothing.

Okay, time to drag out the big guns. I hit the red Panic button, and just like a charm, I heard *Honk! Honk! Honk!* just out of sight. A middle-aged couple turned to stare, and a dog began barking frantically. I just didn't care. I flew down the sidewalk to pass a clump of sesanquas, and there was my car, honking away faithfully. I pressed the Panic button again to silence the horn. Within seconds, I was buckled up and maneuvering the car out of the space I'd wedged it in, thinking all the while about the evening's excursion with the movie people. I was relieved they wouldn't be eating anywhere in town—but Heavenly Barbecue, a huge and popular place on the outskirts of the Lawrenceton side of Atlanta, was often aswarm with locals.

Through a haze of misgiving, I couldn't shake a certain sense of anticipation. I felt like I'd agreed to a date with a rough, sexy guy from the wrong side of the tracks.

It had been a long time since I'd had plans for the evening beyond a dinner with my mother and her new family, or renting a movie to watch with Sally or the Youngbloods. As I worked at the library that afternoon, directing patrons to the right section of the stacks or dealing with the copier (which was at the stage of having to be nursed through every encounter with the public), I thought about my invitation from the movie people much too often. I just had time to shower and change when I left work.

I had to resist the temptation to buy more new clothes. I refused to spend more than five minutes deciding what to put on that evening, but I did check over my chosen shirt and slacks to decide if they needed ironing. As I was frowning at a little crease in my khakis, the telephone rang.

"Uh-huh?" I said into the receiver, my mind a thousand miles away.

"Ms. Teagarden?" The crisp voice could only belong to Patricia Bledsoe, Sam Clerrick's secretary. Patricia the Paragon, as Perry Allison had taken to calling her after she'd found a mistake in his paycheck that cost him money.

"Yes, who's calling?" I didn't want to sound too sure. Why on earth would the woman phone me?

"This is Mrs. Bledsoe," she said, sounding as surprised to be calling as I was to be called.

"What can I do for you?" I asked, trying to modify my voice so my words wouldn't sound abrupt. I'd been at work for seven hours. Why hadn't she taken the opportunity to talk to me then?

"My son Jerome really wants to see the film crew on the job," she said carefully. "Mr. Allison just now told me that you had visited the set this morning. So I was hoping that you could tell me where they are working now."

Patricia Bledsoe also didn't like to use contractions.

I told her the crew had been working at the Episcopalian church that morning, and she checked the address to be sure she knew where that was (there are many, many churches in Lawrenceton, and I am sorry to say there is little racial mixing on Sundays). "But I don't know about tomorrow," I said firmly. "I believe my friend said something about street scenes."

"So they are not likely to be coming to the library?" she asked. I had the odd feeling that Patricia Bledsoe could see the surprised expression on my face, because she added hastily, "That would be so convenient, you see, if he could just come here."

"I have no idea what streets they're going to use," I told her. "I suppose if they wanted to film at the library they would've already asked Sam, either directly or through the City Council."

"That's true," she said. She sounded quite annoyed that she hadn't thought of that herself. "Yes, thank you," she said briskly, and I knew that Patricia was regretting she'd called me at all. "I'm sorry I bothered you, just go back to whatever you were doing," she continued, trying to sound chipper. "Forget I even called."

I thought, *She wishes.*

To my relief, I spotted a familiar tall form in the parking lot. Robin was included in the dinner invitation. I'd been a little anxious at the idea of being alone with a bunch of people I didn't know. Furthermore, they'd be people with whom I had nothing in common. It was pleasant to find out I was only four-sixths right.

Meredith Askew had indeed either lied or been mistaken, because Barrett was standing with the rest beside a rented van. That counterbalanced Robin's presence. Barrett smirked at me, and I felt weary already. The best I could do was to manage my entry into the van, so I climbed in the backseat with Meredith Askew and the assistant to the director, Mark Chesney. Celia was in the middle with Robin, who barely managed to fit his long legs in, and Barrett was in the front passenger seat. The head cameraman, Will Weir, drove. He seemed to be everywhere.

Despite what Meredith had said when she invited me, Celia didn't seem anxious to talk to me, at least not immediately. Mark asked her about her next project. "I'm doing a movie about the sixties radicals," she said. "I play one of those bombers they had then."

After some exclamations from Mark and Will, Celia twisted in her seat to face me directly. "I was in your library the other day," she said. "I really wanted to meet you then, but I ended up checking out some books for research. Now I have my own Lawrenceton, Georgia, library card! Quite a souvenir of the role!"

I smiled faintly and agreed, glad I hadn't been in the library to witness the fuss when she had entered. Celia didn't address me directly after that. She and Meredith chattered back and forth about the industry, and Mark added a comment or two from time to time.

If I'd agreed to come because I wanted to observe *them,* I would have been in hog heaven. As it was, I couldn't escape the feeling that I was out of my element. I found myself thinking of a book I'd left half-read at home and wishing I'd stuck it in my purse so I could pull it out now. But I gave myself a little lecture to get "up" for the occasion. After all, how many chances would I have again to ride in a van with a group of Hollywood insiders?

The answer, to my relief, appeared to be none.

The treatment we got at the restaurant was amazing.

It was like—well, I don't know what it was like. Waiting to greet us at the door was the manager, whose embroidered pocket read "Smoky." Smoky was a short man with a thick thatch of curly, light hair. He was built like a tree trunk, and his heavy, hairy arms waved emphatically as he told us how pleased he was to have us in his establishment. Beaming with pride, he led us to a private room. We had to parade the length of the restaurant to get there. It may have been my imagination, but it seemed to me that Smoky walked quite slowly and mentioned Celia's name—and Barrett's—much more often than necessary.

Once we were seated at a large rectangular table, covered for the occasion with a red paper tablecloth, we were served instantly by a group of favored servers, all of whom yearned desperately to be noticed by someone, anyone, in the magic circle of Hollywood. I had never been waited on with such perkiness, such assiduity. I didn't know whether to jeer or weep.

"Is it always like this?" I whispered to Robin as we were studying our menus.

"Yes," he said, quite matter-of-fact about the spectacle ordinarily normal people were making out of themselves.

There was already a lot to think about.

Robin was at my side because Celia had maneuvered so that that should happen. She sat directly across the table, flanked by Barrett and Will Weir. Meredith and Mark Chesney sat at the ends. The rest of the tables in the private room were empty. The voices of our group sounded unnaturally loud as the menu was discussed with exhaustive—and boring—thoroughness. Robin and I began to talk about our mothers. I'd never met his, but he'd talked about her often and with fondness, and of course he'd met my mother when he lived in Lawrenceton. We kept the conversation going while we placed our orders and received our drinks. That procedure took twice as long since the young people in the Heavenly Barbecue colors (sky blue and deep red) were determined to impress themselves on each and every member of the party; my choice of entrees had never received such attention.

I could see that this was all to impress Celia; somehow, though Celia was not remarkably famous, these young people could tell she was the alpha in our small group. After a few moments' observation, I decided the determining factor wasn't looks; it was attitude.

I acted like no one.

Celia and Meredith were playing the parts of dazzling celebrities who were being just folks, just like everyone else, no special treatment please! Will Weir, who, Robin had whispered, was actually one of the best known and most reliable cameramen in Hollywood, had a definite air of authority that put him firmly in the club, and Robin had a well-known face since he'd promoted his book on so many talk shows. Barrett was handsome, and he looked like an Actor. Mark Chesney and I were the nonentities.

I wish I could say that this was just fine with me, that I hardly noticed it. At least, after five minutes of being mildly chagrined, I worked around to laughing at myself. After that I felt much better. Mark Chesney and I exchanged a smile that let me know he was on my wavelength. Barrett was glowing. I'd never seen him look happier. This evening was apparently a significant one for him, and as I watched him speak to Celia, I wondered if Barrett was attempting a conquest. Robin's claim that he and Celia were no longer a couple seemed to be true; he didn't seem at all concerned that Barrett and Celia were flirting openly and outrageously.

Barrett mentioned his previous visit to Lawrenceton when he was talking about the difficulty some of the cast was having in communicating with the locals. Our accent might be a little heavy to a Midwesterner's ear, I guess.

"You've been to Georgia before?" Meredith asked, as if our state was remote and inaccessible.

"I thought everyone knew," Barrett said. He certainly looked genuinely surprised. "My father lived here."

"He doesn't any longer?" Celia sounded interested and quite innocent.

There was a moment's silence. Barrett and I looked at each other. "No," Barrett said. "Unfortunately, we lost him last year."

Though that made Martin sound like a misaddressed package, I appreciated Barrett's restraint, and I gave him a tiny nod. The subject was dropped, to my relief and, I'll bet, to Barrett's.

Robin and I were discussing the latest book by Robert Crais, whom Robin knew slightly—now, to me that was thrilling—when I became aware that I was being observed. It was like noticing that a mosquito is hovering around your face, a sensation you can't quite pin down and eliminate.

"But the Joe Pike character, how do you think he measures up compared to Hawk in the Parker books?" Robin asked. I was trying to formulate my reply when I glanced across the table and saw that Celia was silent and intent. She was observing me, and even as I looked at her I saw her hand move in a little hand twist that ended with the palm up. I hadn't realized it was a gesture I made often until I saw Celia imitate it.

In a flash, I understood the whole purpose of my being invited along this evening. I could only wonder, in that horrible moment, if Robin had known.

I wanted to get up and walk out of the room and never see any of these people again, because I felt that Celia Shaw had been stealing from me. But in a contrary way, I also wanted to minimize the situation, because I was raised to avoid direct confrontations. Besides, what could I say? "You were copying me?" I hadn't accused anyone of that since the third grade. What could she reply? "Was not!"

"Just trying to get your flavor," Celia explained, looking Sheepish with a capital S. She was playing someone feeling sheepish, rather than actually feeling that way.

"I don't know how you've stood it," I said to Robin, with more frankness than tact. Shoving back my chair and scooping up my purse, I excused myself to go to the Ladies'.

The ladies' room was supposed to look like a barn, God knows why. There were hay bales and corrals, and each "stall" was only shoulder high. Talk about carrying a theme too far. There was no place to be private in there. I stood by the pay phone when I'd emerged, trying to decide who could come get me without asking too many questions. I'd just look like that dreaded thing, a Bad Sport, I finally decided, and stomped back to our private room.

Along the way, a starstruck girl asked me to get Celia Shaw's autograph for her and a man who was trying really hard to look like Johnny Depp told me he could give anyone in that room—male or female—an unforgettable sexual experience. I had no idea what to say to either of them, so I just shook my head.

The food had come while I was gone, and everyone was eating, but there was a testy silence in the room that tipped me off that something had gone wrong while I was out.

I slid into my place and spread my napkin, hoping this wouldn't be the time I'd spill barbecue sauce on my blouse. I don't think I've ever concentrated so hard on eating neatly. Every sixty seconds one of the servers would circulate around the table, asking each person individually if he or she had enough to drink, was satisfied in every way.

I was so self-conscious, thinking of the young woman across from me drinking in my every move and gesture, that I couldn't enjoy a thing. I wished I'd just said to hell with it, and walked right out of the restaurant. I could have called Shelby Youngblood or Sally Allison. Had I been under the spell of Hollywood glamour as much as everyone else? Was that why I'd agreed to come out with these people? I put down my fork with as little noise as I could manage, patted my lips with my napkin, and set it by my plate.

"Ready to leave?" Robin murmured.

"They're not through eating," I whispered.

"We can go," he said. "I called a cab."

"Thanks," I said, realizing as he said it that I wanted to leave more than anything. In a regular speaking voice I thanked Celia for the meal, and though I sounded stiff and hostile I had fulfilled the letter of courtesy. Celia was sulky and on the verge of a tantrum. She muttered something at me. I didn't try to decipher it on the spot; nodding and getting the hell out seemed like the best thing to do.

Robin slid in the cab with me, told the driver where to go, and stared straight ahead.

"Thank you," I said carefully.

"For being there while you were exposed to Celia at her worst?" His voice was dry and brittle. I realized there had been a serious quarrel when I'd left the room. I was petty enough to be glad.

"I guess she was just doing what an actress has to do," I answered, hoping to make him feel less culpable. "Anyway, that was certainly an experience."

"They get so used to being the center of the universe," Robin told me. "I don't think I ever see it as clearly until I see them away from L.A."

I felt uncomfortable. There wasn't a response, so I didn't attempt one.

"She's gotten worse lately," he continued. "She's absentminded, and she forgets her lines. She's…it's like she's going off the tracks, somehow."

I had to tread carefully. No matter if she and Robin had quarreled about how she'd treated me, this woman had been Robin's girlfriend. "Does she use, ah, recreational stuff?" I asked, as delicately as possible.

"Drugs? No. Celia might take a hit off a joint if it's going around, but she doesn't buy it herself and she doesn't take pills."

Somehow, discussing Celia's problems didn't interest me right now, but I felt obliged to listen if Robin wanted to discuss them. Up to a point. But Robin sat in brooding silence all the way to my house, where he told the cab to wait while he walked me to my door. I'd unlocked the door and punched in the security code, he took one step inside.

For a moment I felt awkward, in that lit-up kitchen with a man, alone. Then I thanked Robin for the ride home and for my interesting evening, and he gave a snort that suddenly made me feel at home with him. He seemed much more like my friend Robin than a stranger who'd been living in a strange land. Robin looped one long arm around my shoulders and stooped to give me a kiss on the cheek.

"I'll see you tomorrow," he said.

"No, I have to work."

"You don't want to come back to the set?" He sounded less surprised than he might have a couple of days ago. Robin was reorienting himself to my life.

"No."

Robin looked down at me, his face inscrutable. "Then I'll see you soon," he said finally. I watched as he loped down the steps to cross the yard to the cab waiting on the driveway. There was a car passing by, out on the road, a little unusual for this time of night. Maybe my neighbor Clement had been out late.

What a strange evening it had been. I fed Madeleine and trudged up the stairs, yawning hard enough to make a cracking sound. As I got ready for bed, going through my usual skin and stretching routine, I wondered if I should have foregone my evening out with the movie people. Then I thought, *That's a once-in-a-lifetime experience. Even if I didn't enjoy it at all, it's a good thing to have done.* I was glad it was over, though, and as I composed myself to sleep I thought of Celia Shaw's clever, sulky, beautiful face. I wondered if she'd ever win an Oscar; I could say I'd known her when.

That would be more fun than knowing her now.

Five

Making a liar out of me, the next morning saw me on my way back to the movie set, which today, I'd discovered, was the Sparling County Courthouse. I was still blinking and trying to feel completely alert. Beside me in the front seat was my friend Angel Youngblood: mother, stuntwoman, and former bodyguard. Pregnancy and motherhood had not had any visible effect on Angel's long, sleek body.

When the phone had rung at the crack of dawn, Angel's was the last voice I'd expected to hear. "Hey, Roe," she'd said, her flat Florida drawl instantly recognizable. "Listen, I need some help."

"What?" I knew I sounded groggy, and I tried to focus on the clock. It was six, time for me to get up and get ready for work.

"Sorry I woke you up."

"No, no, I have to get ready for work anyway. What can I do for you?" Angel never called without a reason; she wasn't a chatterer.

"Shelby's already at work with his car, mine won't start, and I need to leave the baby-sitter hers because Joan's got a doctor's appointment today. Can you give me a lift to the movie set?"

I ran a hand over my face, and recalled that Angel had told me she'd gotten work on the set. "Sure," I said. "I'll be there in thirty minutes or less."

"Thanks." Angel hung up.

I washed my face and brushed my teeth, pulled on a long, pale orange tee-shirt style dress and a light sweater, slid into some clogs, powdered my face, and clattered down the stairs and out the front door before I had really attained consciousness. I was a little more alert by the time I beeped the horn outside Angel and Shelby's ranch-style home.

Angel slid out of the front door like a thief in the night, her Capri-length black stretch pants and her white blouse emphasizing her golden colors and smooth body movements. Her thick blond hair was caught back in a ponytail, and she wore no makeup, which was Angel's norm.

"How's Joan?" I asked as Angel climbed into the car.

Angel grinned, and went from looking serious and possibly dangerous to looking like a mother who was proud as hell of the most wonderful baby in the world. "She's into banging on pots and pans," Angel told me, and we talked about Joan's progress for a minute or two. "My neighbor is keeping her today. She has a little boy a couple of months older. Courthouse," she reminded me, and as I pulled away from the curb to go to Lawrenceton's fake-antebellum edifice, she began to tell me about a civil confrontation Shelby had had with Martin's replacement at the Pan-Am Agra plant.

I was listening with great interest, when I stood back and gave myself a hard look. Was I that dreary cliché, the hometown honey? I found the Hollywood people boring, compared to Angel's fascinating account of little Joan's first crawling. Maybe I was pulling a double cross on myself, pretending enthrallment with family scenes of the Youngbloods to hide my secret lust for the Hollywood way of life?

It was both a relief and a slight disappointment to touch the bottom of my well of self-absorption and find I was absolutely sincere in my preference for the small details of home. And I was definitely getting a little too fond of my own navel, I concluded. So I concentrated on listening to every single thing Angel told me. I even volunteered to baby-sit Joan one evening so Angel and Shelby could go out together. Angel rolled her eyes at me doubtfully, but agreed to talk to Shelby about my offer.

Today the trailers and cables and cameras—all the paraphernalia I'd seen yesterday—had been set up in a new location, the front yard of the courthouse. Even the Molly's Moveable Feasts van was there, with its table set up and attended by the same auburn-headed young woman. (If she was actually Molly, who was doing the cooking?) Today the table was spread with pitchers of juice and doughnuts, and a plate of fruit. I wondered, for the first time, how long the movie people would actually have to stay in town.

Robin had told me that most of the shots filmed in Lawrenceton would be exteriors. Sets would be built back at the studio for interior scenes. So maybe scenes dealing with the trial were being shot today? I wondered why on earth they'd need a stuntwoman, and decided maybe it would be better not to ask.

For the first time, as Angel scanned the street for some safe parking spot, I thought of how difficult it would be to be an actor, to have to imagine how your character would've changed as a result of scenes you hadn't shot yet. You'd have to figure out how the character would react after some of the events in the film, before you'd ever emotionally experienced them. There was more to this acting than met the eye.

I had intended to drop Angel off and go on my way, but she knew one of the women working in the crew and wanted to introduce me. The friend, Carolina Venice, was one of the makeup artists working in a big trailer a little west of the courthouse. Angel's friend looked as exotic as her name. Easily five feet eleven, Carolina Venice had a smoking habit, cornrowed and beaded hair, and multiple piercings. The lip and tongue decorations made me a little queasy, I have to confess, though the woman was as warm and welcoming as she could be.

"Give me fifteen minutes," she said. "I have to finish this woman, and then I'll be with you. Here, settle into these chairs." There were two cheap lawn chairs on the rolling platform (with steps built in) that had been pushed up to the makeup trailer.

I perched on one, looking around me to see if I could spy Robin. I felt a certain need to explain why I was where I'd said I would never go again. I was just yards away from Celia's trailer—at least I was pretty sure it was the same one Celia had used the day before. Will Weir, pulling on a lightweight jacket, was saying something over his shoulder to (I presumed) Celia, nodding, as he shut the door. Everyone I saw had the Styrofoam cups of coffee and juice that Molly's Moveable Feasts was handing out. Mark Chesney went to the door of the trailer and knocked, but hurried away after a moment. I wasn't close enough to hear what response he'd gotten. A young woman I didn't know darted up to the door, cracked it slightly, and called something inside. Then she darted away as quickly as she'd come. I was interrupted in my study of movie location movement patterns by the emergence of Carolina, who'd had time to get pumped up about talking to her old friend.

She hugged Angel, shrieked at pictures of the baby, asked after Shelby, and behaved exactly like a happily reunited friend, gold hoops or no gold hoops. After a minute, it was easy to forget her bizarre appearance and respond to her warmth and cheer.

When the two were deep into reminiscence, I decided I could use some orange juice. I strolled over to the laden table.

"Can I pour you some coffee?" asked the young woman. She had discarded one white coat and was pulling on another. I was willing to bet that white coats had a high turnover. While I picked up a cup of juice, I noticed that she was prettier close-up. Her dark red hair was thick and smooth, her skin was clear, and her eyes were a nice blue. It was her heavy jaw that threw her face off balance and prevented her from being really attractive. The embroidered name on her white jacket read "Tracy."

"So you're not Molly," I remarked.

She laughed. "No, no. Molly's the genius. I'm just the server. When I clean this table up, it'll be time for Molly to come with the bag lunches for the crew. Then when I clear those away, it'll be afternoon snack time."

"You must get to know everyone who works here."

"By sight, anyway," she agreed. "They're all pretty cool. In this kind of weather, this is a great job." Kind of a dead-end one, I would have thought, but on a beautiful clear day in October in a lovely town like Lawrenceton, with an interesting scene to watch, the idea didn't seem so terrible.

"Who do you like best?" I asked idly.

"Oh, the writer." Tracy's face, already high-colored,

flushed a deeper red. "I've read everything Robin's ever written. I've got first editions of every book, all signed."

She sounded like an ardent reader to me. "He's good," I agreed, trying not to smile.

"I saw you talking to him yesterday," Tracy said. "You known him long?"

"Yes, several years," I said. "Of course, Robin lived here at the time of the murders, and so did I."

"You wouldn't be...you couldn't be...Aurora Teagarden?" She looked absolutely dazed.

"Yes, I am," I said, trying not to flinch.

"OhmiGod, this is amazing," she shrieked. "To actually meet you!"

Oh, boy. High time to haul ass out of there, I figured. I finished my cup of juice, thanked Tracy, and tossed my cup into the large, lined garbage can, brimming over with identical cups and napkins and paper plates. Tracy immediately bundled up the contents, secured the bag with a twisty, and tossed it into the back of the catering van. By the time I went to say good-bye to Carolina and Angel, she had already relined the can and bundled her dirty coat and some dish towels into the van as well.

The two friends were still on the porch. They'd laid claim to the lawn chairs, and people who moved in and out of the makeup trailers had to work around them. Carolina was on her second or third cigarette, and she was telling Angel something between puffs. Angel was listening with some intensity. I was a little shy about interrupting, even though all I wanted to do was tell Angel I was leaving, so I looked around me, trying to look like I was content rather than impatient.

I was surprised to see Meredith Askew tripping along in my direction. She was smiling, a sort of conciliatory wincing lifting of the lips.

"Ms. Teagarden," she said while she was still a few feet away. "Celia told me last night that if you showed up today, she hoped you would come talk to her a second." She came to a halt below the porch.

"You're her messenger, now?" I asked, noting that my voice was appropriately cool.

Meredith's smile might have twitched a little, but she kept her composure up. "Just doing a friend a favor," she said, her voice level. "Celia would like to apologize for her...for last night."

Over Meredith's head I could see Barrett going into Celia's trailer. He'd knocked while he stood on the top step, and if he'd gotten an answer I hadn't been able to hear it from where I stood, maybe eighteen feet away. He looked puzzled, knocked again. He cracked the door, called "Celia?" loudly enough for me to hear. He opened the door and stepped in, his face troubled.

I was just congratulating myself on Barrett's not noticing me when he stumbled right back out of Celia's trailer, his hand over his mouth. When I saw Barrett, I lost track of the conversations going on around me. I know trouble when I see it.

I glanced around the set, hoping someone else would

come to Barrett's aid; he was so obviously sick, and something terrible had so obviously happened. I had a sinking feeling in the pit of my stomach that told me I wouldn't be getting to work on time today. As I watched, Barrett groped his way to the end of the trailer and bent over, one hand supporting himself against the side, retching.

For a second of blazing anger, I wondered if all these people weren't *acting* as though they hadn't seen Barrett. For all their attention to each other and their jobs, not one person appeared to have registered that there was a problem.

I went down the steps, bypassed Meredith, and approached my stepson warily. "What's happened?" I asked him.

He didn't seem surprised to see me, or angry, so I knew with even more surety that something was very wrong.

"She's dead in there," he gasped, and he began heaving again.

"Celia…is dead?" I could hear my own voice sharpen and rise with incredulity. I started to say, "Are you sure?" but then I realized that was pretty damn insulting.

"Go get Joel," he moaned.

I wondered if my stepson thought the director could actually bring his leading lady back to life.

"I'll get him," Carolina said from behind me. "I know where he is."

"What did he say?" I heard Meredith ask her. "What did Barrett say?"

I moved over to the open door of the trailer and peeked in. I didn't even put my foot on the concrete block that served as a step.

Celia was half-lying on the couch, up against one wall. The stack of books—including some library books—and the manuscript were tossed around her feet, which were flat on the floor. A dark red throw cushion, stained and nasty, lay on the couch beside her. Her tongue protruded a little from her mouth. It looked bruised, as well. There was a big dent in her forehead.

The Emmy was on the couch beside her. Its base was not clean.

Celia was definitely deceased. Feeling quite wobbly myself, I shut the door and leaned my back against it. I didn't want anyone else to see what I'd seen.

"What is it, Roe?" Angel had loped over and was looking at me quizzically. "Don't tell me she's dead. That's what Barrett keeps saying." Angel really, really didn't want anything to be wrong, but there was no help for it. I had to tell her.

Carolina returned. "He's on the way," she reported.

"You might want to call a doctor. Did the crew bring one?" I asked. She shook her head and her heavy earrings, too many to count, swayed as her head moved. Carolina's skull gleamed dully in the early-morning sun as she pulled a cell phone out of her pocket. It was the thinnest cell phone I'd ever seen. She dialed 911 as I watched. While she was speaking to the dispatcher who answered, Joel Park Brooks suddenly appeared in front of me as if he'd been expelled from another dimension. Mark Chesney was dogging his heels.

"What's this you say?" he asked, mad as hell at me.

In a cowardly way, I nodded my head toward Barrett.

"Oh my God, Joel," Barrett said weakly. He'd dropped to his knees and was pressing his face with both hands as if to force the grief out of it. "Celia is dead. She died some awful way."

As if I were a fly, Joel Park Brooks took me by the shoulder and shoved me aside. Before I could stop him, he flung open the trailer door. Leaping up the step into the trailer, he bent over Celia. Meredith and Mark were peering through the door, too. Both of them stood with one hand pressed against the door frame, on opposite sides. Altogether, the movie people were doing a great job of destroying evidence.

And I heard the voice I'd been dreading to hear, Robin's.

"What's wrong, Roe?" he asked.

"I'm so sorry," I said, almost whispering. I wanted to be a hundred miles away.

"What's happened?" Robin's voice got louder as his fear mounted.

"She's dead," Barrett said. "I can't believe it, but she's dead. We spent last night together, and now she's dead."

"What did you say?" Robin bellowed, and I crouched down.

"We..." All of a sudden, Barrett seemed to realize that this was neither the time nor the place nor the best choice of confidant. "Forget it, man," he muttered, but there were many ears clustering around by that point, including mine, and if Barrett had truly wanted to keep this intimate knowledge to himself, it was too late by thirty seconds.

That helped me pull myself together more than anything.

I moved over to my stepson, and laid my hand on his arm. He looked at me, too distraught to be hostile. "Barrett," I said, as quietly and earnestly as I could, "Don't say anything else. Everyone is listening. The police will be here soon."

"An ambulance," he began, and then closed his mouth with a snap.

"We called 911. But it's not gonna do her any good, and you know it. That woman was killed," I told him, keeping my voice even and low.

"Murdered?" he said, way too loud. I could see cell phones spring up right, left, and sideways.

"Quiet, Barrett. Yes, she was murdered. I'd keep my mouth shut, if I were you."

Anger flashed across his handsome face, followed by intense thought. Barrett was certainly good at projecting his changing emotions.

"What did you say?" Robin was standing to Barrett's side, his fists clenched.

"I was just talking. Ignore me." Barrett turned to walk away.

As if I weren't there, Robin spun Barrett around and

clamped both his hands on Barrett's shoulders. Barrett was younger than Robin by around fifteen years, but he was shorter, and Robin had a pretty good grip. I was going to have to believe Robin hadn't disengaged from his affair with Celia as much as he'd thought.

The movie people on the set were milling around, and I could hear sirens coming closer. But everyone there seemed to see his or her role as that of spectator, rather than participant. Robin opened his mouth to yell at Barrett, and Barrett's eyes ignited with anger, and I cast around for someone to help me.

Of course! Angel Youngblood met my eyes and moved behind Barrett, while I got behind Robin and circled him with my arms and pulled. Someone behind me actually laughed, and I resolved to track down who that was and kick him in the shins. I know I am small, and I know Robin is tall, but I was not in the mood for amusement.

Robin actually struggled for a minute, but I clung like a barnacle, and when he realized who it was had ahold of him, he relaxed. Blocked by his body from seeing what progress Angel had made with Barrett, I pulled gently on Robin's arms to get him to take a few steps away. He came willingly, and I could see that the anger had drained out of him. Robin wrapped his long arms around me and pulled me close, bowing his head over mine and crying.

For once I wished I were taller. I would put his face in the hollow of my neck and let him cry there, concealed, if only I could. I stood on tiptoes to let him lean on me more comfortably, and I patted his back. I wondered if I had any tissues in my purse, a soft mesh shoulder bag that was now banging uncomfortably on my bottom.

Will Weir was sitting on the curb of the sidewalk, his head buried in his hands. Meredith Askew was slumped by him, her makeup a mess, her hair all tangled. She was sitting as close to Will as she could get without climbing in his lap. Joel Park Brooks began shrieking at someone a few yards away. I recognized his voice, though I couldn't see him for the cloud of people, all chattering away on their phones.

"Hang up the damn cell phone," he screamed, and a Motorola whizzed past me. Then a wafer-thin red phone. Everyone moved back in a hurry to protect their property from the director's hands, and there was a flurry of clicks as people hid their cells. I glimpsed Carolina sliding hers down the front of her tee shirt. Unless I missed my bet, Joel Park Brooks would be in no hurry to go after that one.

"Robin," I said, hesitating to break into his grief.

He lifted his head and looked down at me. I reached up to rub a tear off his face. "She was so fragile," he said. "She was such a mess."

Not "I loved her," or "What will I do without her?"

I pushed my glasses back on my nose and eyed him doubtfully.

"I'm really sorry, Robin, but the police are here. We

need to find somewhere for you to wait, because they're going to want to talk to you."

"Did you say," he began slowly, disregarding what I'd told him, "Did you say Celia had been murdered?"

"I'm sorry, yes."

He looked baffled. "But that doesn't make any sense," he said.

It seemed like a strange comment. But just as I opened my mouth to ask him what he'd meant, I heard a familiar voice.

And the day got even worse.

Six

His round blue eyes went from me, up to Robin, over to Barrett, and back again. "Isn't this fascinating," said Detective Arthur Smith. It was a moment pregnant with emotions, but those emotions were so snarled up it would have been hard to tease them apart.

If I just explain that my history with Arthur is long and complicated, it will spare us all a lot of tedium.

I hadn't seen Arthur (to speak to) in almost two years; of course, in a town the size of Lawrenceton, it would be hard to avoid glimpses of him, and I hadn't particularly been trying to do that.

Arthur was somewhat burlier than he had been in the days when we'd dated, and his hair was a little thinner, it seemed to me. He was still a solid block of a man, with hard blue eyes and curly pale hair. These past few months I'd been so far out of the loop that I realized I didn't even know if Lynn (Arthur's ex) and their little girl were still living in town.

"Who is this?" he asked me, as casually as if we'd had coffee together the hour before. He was pointing at my stepson.

"This is Barrett Bartell, Martin's son. He found her."

Arthur squatted down in front of Barrett. Barrett met his eyes. I could tell Barrett was enough his father's son to dislike Arthur on sight—but Barrett was involved in a murder now, and couldn't afford such an emotion. I squeezed his arm to warn him. Barrett was definitely snapping back into his personality. He yanked away from me, and he didn't do it subtly.

I tried not to feel hurt, but it didn't work. I felt mostly…tired, I guess. I struggled to rise above it. Martin would want me to help Barrett, whether Barrett wanted to be helped or not.

"What brought you to Miss Shaw's trailer this morning?" Arthur said. His voice didn't sound particularly friendly.

"I needed to talk to her about…" And then Barrett stopped in mid-sentence.

"About what?"

He looked like he'd just seen the Ghost of You Better Shut Your Mouth over Arthur's shoulder, and it had shaken its finger at him.

"He was going to talk to Celia about the implications of their having spent the night together," Robin said, his face absolutely expressionless. I had no idea what he was thinking or how he was feeling. Somehow he maintained his composure and straightened his slumped shoulders, his face now in profile to me and once more under guard. It was a "man" thing to do, I thought wryly. But I admired him for holding on to his personality under the pressure of the shock and grief…and anger—he must be feeling. Even if he and Celia were no longer involved, it had to sting that she had so quickly found someone else to fill her bed.

Will Weir stepped over to Robin and put a hand on his shoulder. For a second the two men embraced, and if ever I had seen two miserable people, this was the occasion. Then they let each other go, and I was glad Robin had someone to comfort him, someone who'd known the dead girl well.

"Why are *you* here?" Arthur asked me. I had the feeling he'd said it more than once.

"Yeah, Mom," Barrett said jeeringly. He'd recovered far more quickly than I'd hoped he would. His defenses were firmly back in place. "You come to check up on me? I thought you'd had enough of us movie people last night."

Martin had put up with a lot from Barrett, but if he'd heard Barrett speak to me this way, he would've knocked his son from here to kingdom come. I knew that as well as I knew my own name; and Barrett knew it, too. I met his eyes to see if there was any shame lurking there. There was, but it wasn't enough.

The guilt-engendered protective feeling I'd had for

the young man—which I likened to temporary insanity—dropped right off my shoulders. Inside my head, I informed Martin that his son was just going to have to fend for himself. "And it's about damn time," I muttered, telling Martin a posthumous home truth.

"What?" Arthur looked startled, as well he might.

"I had hoped," I said slowly, "that you would make your father proud." Barrett looked as if I'd kicked him in the jewels. "Surely, Barrett, you're thinking more about this poor, dead young woman than you are about your little personal issues with me." I turned my back on Martin's son. I felt thirty years older than Barrett, rather than ten.

I decided to pretend he wasn't there. "Angel's car wouldn't start, so I brought her to work today," I explained to Arthur, who'd been listening to my exchange with Barrett with great attention. "She wanted me to meet her friend, the pretty woman with all the earrings, over there." I inclined my head in Carolina's direction. "Then, Celia's friend Meredith came to get me, to tell me Celia wanted to apologize for her behavior last night."

"What behavior?" Arthur asked, which was a reasonable question. But I didn't want to talk about my vulnerability to Celia's particular sort of—well, maybe "cruelty" was too severe a word—she'd *used* me…I got mad all over again, and lost my train of thought entirely.

"What did Celia Shaw do last night?" Arthur said gently. He had prompted me without being asked, an unpleasant reminder of how well he knew me. He reached out as if he were going to take my hand, and then changed the movement to a hair-smoothing gesture.

I cinched up my pride. "She invited me to dinner so she could observe my mannerisms," I said. I cut my eyes sideways to see if Barrett was going to comment, but he'd turned away.

"How did you find the deceased this morning?" Arthur asked. He'd gotten out his little notebook and the cheap Bic pen he preferred. He was still using the same model. Didn't make any difference if he lost it, he'd always told me.

"While I was talking to Meredith, I saw Barrett knock at the trailer door, open it, and go in. He came out looking sick." I shrugged, letting him know that was that. "Other people had come up to the trailer earlier and talked to her."

"I'll talk to you later, Roe," he said. "You wait over there." He pointed to one of the folding chairs on the porch of the makeup trailer. I didn't wait for a second offer. I sat in the chair and crossed my legs and took a few deep breaths. I was glad I'd worn a dress, a cool dress. The sun was coming up and the touch of it on my skin was beginning to show that little kiss of ferocity that said the temperature was going to reach the eighties. October is truly unpredictable in the South. I slid out of my sweater.

I got out my own cell phone and called the library to explain why I'd be late. Sam's assistant, Patricia Bledsoe, was at her desk, and as correct as ever. What a pain in the patootie that woman was, I thought absently, and then felt embarrassed at myself. Since when had dressing and speaking correctly, and acting professional, been a pain? "I'll try to be in this afternoon," I told Patricia and snapped my phone shut.

Well, it was a pain. She was a pain. And she was hiding something, my less correct self insisted on muttering to my nicer, more charitable persona. The last thing in the world Patricia Bledsoe would want was her Jerome hanging around on a movie set. That whole conversation had been fishy.

"I should have known not to bring you this morning," a familiar voice said dryly, and Angel folded her long legs to sit beside my chair.

"It's not my fault stuff happens. Celia Shaw's dead," I said.

"I heard tell."

"I don't think it was a natural death. Unless she had fits or something. But then, someone whacked her with the Emmy."

"Ummm."

"Barrett found the body."

"Time Barrett grew up."

"I bet Barrett wouldn't be such a…" I groped for a nice way to say it.

"Asshole," Angel supplied.

"Asshole, if Martin had stayed with Barrett's mother." Sometimes the blunt term fits the bill best.

"I bet not." Angel began braiding her hair, her slim muscular arms stretched back behind her head. "I bet he would've been *worse*. Martin was miserable with his first wife. Named Cindy, right? Shelby met her—long, long time ago. I know you got to know her a little last winter, but I think she must have mellowed out by then." Angel secured her braid with an elastic band.

"So it's not just me who thinks Barrett is hard to deal with?" I felt a little better.

"Oh, no." Angel was matter-of-fact. "Shelby, little as he knows him, can't stand to see that boy coming. And he *is* still a boy, when he should be a man."

It was so refreshing to have a conversation with someone who agreed with me, and wouldn't think the less of me for detesting my stepson. I began to feel a few degrees less tense. Then I thought of the crumpled body just a few yards away, and realized that it was pretty darn likely someone had killed Celia Shaw while I was sitting in this very chair. I shuddered, despite the gathering heat.

"Wonder what this'll do to the movie schedule." Angel took a sip from a bottle of water she'd snagged from the catering table.

"They won't cancel, surely?"

"No, they'll just hire someone else, I figure."

"Meredith Askew?"

"That would be unusual," Angel said. "I think they'll hire someone just about Celia's level, and Celia was several steps higher on the food chain than Meredith."

I forgot, all too often, that Angel had an eclectic background that included considerable knowledge of the movie world. She was the most down-to-earth person I'd ever met, and I admired her many abilities immensely. And I would much rather think about that than the dent in Celia Shaw's forehead.

"Meredith's going to hope she'll be moved up," Angel went on, spotting the young woman in the crowd, making the most of the "friend of the deceased" role. "But I doubt it."

I thought about that a little. "So, someone's going to be mighty happy about Celia dying."

Angel nodded. "But no telling who that is, though there may have been some other woman who's been on the back burner the whole time, some woman we don't know about. Carolina told me that Celia had been acting strange for the few days they'd been here."

"Robin thought so, too," I said after a moment. I had seen the perplexity on his face while he observed his former flame. I remembered the previous morning, when it had seemed for all the world as though Celia was going to slap the director.

"So that's Robin Crusoe, over there?" Angel had come to Lawrenceton after Robin left. She gestured with one bony finger, and I nodded, glad she'd spotted him for me.

Robin looked haggard, understandably enough, since he'd just discovered his former flame had been murdered, and that she'd spent the night before her death with another man. He'd put on dark glasses and was talking to a middle-aged woman with gray-streaked black hair. Robin pushed his fingers up under his glasses, and I knew he was brushing away tears. I pushed my own glasses up on my nose.

"You and him were tight?"

"Kind of," I said, feeling unaccountably shy about it. "But we're talking years ago. Right before I dated Arthur Smith." I looked down at my hands, and began twisting my wedding band around on the finger it no longer fit.

Angel raised a blond eyebrow. "So, what happened with Robin?"

"I was really fond of him. I think he was fond of me, too. But when he decided to write a book about the murders, and I realized there was no way he could leave me out of the book, I felt pretty unhappy about it. And when he went to Hollywood with his agent to push the book proposal, our connection just kind of tapered off."

"He call you?"

"Oh…yeah. At first."

"When did he quit?"

"When I told him I was marrying Martin."

"And then he moved on to that Celia Shaw?"

"That's what the gossip magazines said. I think they had pretty much called it quits by the time they got here."

"So he moved from the real you to the play you." Angel looked amused at my wince. After a second of considering that unnerving idea, I shrugged.

We fell silent and watched the unfolding panorama together. Joel Park Brooks, shaved head flashing in the sun, was being attended by paramedics, by Mark, and by several other people whose names and functions I had not yet learned. He seemed to feel that the FBI should be brought in to investigate the death of an important actress like Celia Shaw. The Hollywood dispensation, I guess.

Robin had found a chair and sunk down onto it, his hands on his knees, lost in thought. I wondered if I should go to him.

Meredith Askew, still looking properly distraught, was resting her face on the shoulder of Chip Brodnax, the tall young man who was portraying Robin. His back was to me, so I had a good view of Meredith's face. As I watched, I saw her expression change to one of intense speculation. She was staring into the distance, unaware that anyone was observing her. As if she'd turned to me and spoken her thoughts out loud, I could tell that she was wondering if she had a chance of replacing Celia in the main role.

This was depressing. If anyone in this crowd (besides possibly Robin) was simply grieving for Celia Shaw, I could see no sign of it.

"Let's us go," I suggested to Angel.

"Won't the police get us?"

"I have a feeling I can get around that."

I made my way through the crowd to Arthur, who was issuing instructions to three other cops. I waited until he'd finished speaking, and as soon as they scattered to do his bidding, I knew he would turn to me.

"What can I do for you?" he asked.

"Can Angel and I go home?"

"Will you stay at your house until I come later? Will you not talk to anyone else?"

"I promise."

"Okay, then. You and Angel can go."

"Thanks." I tried to dredge up a smile for him, but I couldn't.

I trudged back to Angel and gave her the thumbs-up. We made our way to my car and climbed back in. Though it was only nine o'clock, it seemed like a lifetime since we'd gotten to the set. The day was getting hotter by the minute. The car was stuffy. The streets around the movie site were almost chaotic; I had never in my life seen traffic this disordered in Lawrenceton. I figured all the police had been grabbed off traffic control and shifted to the murder scene. It wouldn't take the news crews long to get there, especially with all the busy cell phones on the set. I was willing to bet CNN already knew about it, had maybe aired a bulletin, if Celia rated that high.

I decided not to turn on the radio. I didn't want to hear anything about the murder, I didn't want to listen to any music, I didn't want to know the weather report. I just wanted to get out of here. With Angel helping me avoid cars and people, all going places they shouldn't go, I finally drove out of the area. I made a huge effort to obey every traffic rule. I was so grateful to Arthur for letting us leave, I was determined to be no trouble at all.

Once I got away from the town center, traffic thinned out dramatically. I took the county highway that led northeast out of town, past the very nice suburb where my mother and her husband live. My house is about a mile out of town, on a road that turns into farms pretty much right after it leaves the city limits.

The house waited for me, silent and dim, perfectly clean.

Angel hadn't been out to the house in a while. She looked around, a curious expression on her narrow face. She moved down the hall with her quiet grace, looking from side to side like a cat exploring unfamiliar territory.

"Geez," she said finally, "I want to kick the walls just to make a scuff mark. How can you live like this?"

"I don't know how to live any other way," I said. And it was the first time that way struck me as odd. I stood in the middle of the long hall that runs from the front door and past the stairs down to a closet door, looked to the left into the formal living room, and I felt weirdly isolated. I stood, in my orange knit dress, feeling the coolness of the house, the shadows cast by the bright morning sun streaming in the windows, the sudden lack of contrast when clouds floated across the sun. I felt time passing.

"Do you ever have company?" she asked.

"No. At least, very seldom. But you know," I said,

pondering this idea through, "That's not actually my fault. People don't come to see me. Even when I say, 'Come by and see me,' they don't."

"You need to move back into town," Angel said, her voice flat and definite.

I gaped at her. "Like that would be easy! Like moving isn't incredibly stressful!"

She cocked her head, her blond braid trailing to one side.

"Is living like this *relaxing?* This place is a tomb."

I stared at her, shocked.

She was absolutely right.

It was the second revelatory moment I'd had in two days.

"I would help," she offered. "I could bring Joan's playpen and set it up, and she'd be good for a while."

"But this house," I said, feeling my tears spring up. "I was so happy here. Martin bought it for me."

"You think Martin would like you being here by yourself? You think Martin would ever live in a place this...dead?"

That cut me to the quick. Martin had surrounded himself with energy, with projects, with life. I felt instantly that I had failed him, yet again.

"You didn't die with Martin," Angel said brutally.

I gasped in surprise at the way her thought chimed in on what I was thinking. "This house has so many memories," I said feebly.

"You have the memories inside you. This house is

stifling you. It's too big, it's out of the way, and it's... unwelcoming."

"Enough," I said.

Wisely, Angel did keep silent. We went to the kitchen, and I got out two glasses and filled them with ice while Angel got the pitcher of tea out of the refrigerator. Angel poured, and I put a package of Sweet 'N Low in mine.

In a desperate way, it hurt to even consider leaving this house. I had sure had enough hurting. But, with very little inner debate, I found I was thinking that Angel was right.

To effect such a change seemed incredibly daunting. I began to break it down into steps.

I would have to find a house in town. That would be easy, with a mother in real estate.

I'd have to have everything in this house packed and ready to move. I could afford to have that done for me.

I would have to sell this house. Well, part of keeping the house perfect was having its contents pared down to the minimum. This house was ready to show, as it was. With all the improvements I'd made, I had no doubt it would find a buyer sooner or later.

I'd have to pay someone to move all the furniture and boxes to the new house. So, the biggest exertion would be unpacking in the new house.

When I'd first met Angel and Shelby, they'd been hired by Martin to help bring this house to renovated life. They'd helped make the move into the house as smooth and painless as such a major upheaval could be. Now, Angel was offering to help me move out of the house. Somehow, tying the two events together made me cry. In the past year, I'd become used to sudden outbreaks of tears, but it startled Angel. I had to wave a reassuring hand at her, to let her know I was going to be all right. She eyed me doubtfully, but she relaxed when she realized she didn't have to figure out how to comfort me.

She indicated the phone and raised her eyebrows, and I nodded. Shelby now had his own office at Pan-Am Agra, and she was busy relating the events of the morning to him as I strolled out of the room and across the hall into the den to get a Kleenex. I kicked off my sandals, put my ice-tinkling glass on the small table by my current book. I folded my legs under me as I settled in the large leather armchair that had been Martin's favorite. I hadn't slept well the night before, and the day so far had been exhausting. When the air-conditioning came on again, with its relaxing drone, it seemed only natural to lay my head against the wing of the chair and close my eyes.

Seven

There was a hand holding mine. It felt comfortable; long, thin, fingers twined through my short ones. I opened my eyes to see Robin in front of me, sitting on the ottoman that matched the chair.

"Was I snoring?" I asked.

"No, actually. Just sitting there like you were resting your eyes for a minute."

I pushed my glasses up with one finger. "Where's Angel?"

"She's out spraying a wasp nest. What an energetic woman. If I were left alone in this house, I'd head for the bookshelves." The shelves I'd had put in all up and down the hall were my favorite feature, too.

"Angel's not much one for reading," I said. "You're welcome to go to the shelves if you want. How come you're here? I'm glad you are," I added hastily, not wanting to be rude, "but I'm kind of surprised Arthur let you come."

"Luckily for me, I had an alibi for this morning."

"Oh?"

"First, I ate breakfast in the hotel restaurant at the same time as at least ten other people. It's quite the local watering hole, huh? Then, I was on the phone with my agent for thirty minutes. We were talking about this film, and the contract for my next two books. Then, after I got to the set, Joel grabbed me to discuss some dialogue changes. So I think I'm pretty well covered."

"That's lucky for you. So Arthur said you could come out here?"

"No, I just came out here on my own." There was a pause, not an uncomfortable one.

"Angel was telling me I should move," I said.

"How do you feel about that?"

"I was thinking I was staying here because I had been happy here." I was still a little simple from my nap.

"And now you think?"

"I think Angel is maybe right." I wiggled straight in the chair, untwisted my legs. I was too old to fall asleep in such a position without paying a penalty. "I loved this house the moment I saw it, and I've loved living in it. And I've spent a mint on it. But now it just feels… empty." I made a face. "Like I'm not even here any more."

"Would you live somewhere else?"

"You mean, leave Lawrenceton?" I'd wondered what

would happen if Martin got transferred, so this wasn't a new idea. "Not likely. Not if I don't have to."

"So you'd look for another house in town?"

"Yes." Come to think of it, it was true that I could live anywhere in the world I wanted. I could live in England. I could travel to Italy. But that idea of moving out of my normal orbit scared the heck out of me. I was okay, right here in Lawrenceton. I knew who I was, here. And the time might be coming when my mother would need me; she never had, but it was always possible.

I'd always had the feeling I was a frill, rather than a necessity, for my mother.

Robin was looking thoughtful, but not as traumatized as I'd expected.

"Do you feel very bad?" I asked, trying to keep my voice small and level. After all, his former companion had just been murdered, and she'd spent the night with someone else before that, to boot. A punch in the stomach and a kick in the privates, all at the same time.

"I don't feel like you'd think," Robin said ambiguously. He took his hand back and raked it through his hair, which was long enough to get seriously rumpled.

"Oh? And how would I think you'd feel?"

"You'd think I'd feel like you did when you lost Martin."

"No, I wouldn't."

"Why not?"

"Because I really loved Martin, and you didn't love

Celia." And then I closed my eyes and put my hand over my mouth, because I never should have said that.

Robin didn't speak, and I opened my eyes just a sliver to take a peek at his face. He looked sad. He didn't look heartbroken.

"I guess not," he said, looking down at his hands, dangling between his knees. "It was great for a while, but the last few months, I've been feeling like she was keeping secrets from me."

"Secrets? What kind?"

Robin raised his eyebrows at me so I'd elaborate.

"Like…an 'I'm pregnant' kind of secret, or an 'I know who stole the nuclear warhead,' or 'I was witness to a mob rubout'?"

Robin almost smiled. "I think it was more in the personal category."

"Did you notice anything different about her?"

"Yes," he said, as though he'd just realized that. "Yes, there was a lot different about her. Sometimes she seemed like she was staring into space, not even in the same dimension. Sometimes she'd fall."

I remembered seeing Celia stumble in the parking lot of Great Day.

"It was like she wasn't always in control of her own body. I suspected she was using drugs, for a while, but I'd never seen a recreational drug affect anyone quite like that. And I never saw her using, never."

Her hand flying out to graze Joel's cheek, her horrified face…

"So maybe she was ill. Maybe she did die of some natural cause?" That would be great for those of us among the living. Though it sure hadn't looked natural to me. Could she have had some kind of fit?

"The police don't think so. But maybe they just have to act like it's a homicide, until they know different."

"Did you tell Arthur all this that we've talked about?"

"No, he was more interested in establishing where I'd been all morning. He did tell me he wanted to talk to me again later, not to leave town. As if I would."

I sat forward in my chair, preparatory to getting up to head to the bathroom. Not only did I need the facilities, I needed to rinse out my mouth and brush my hair. I had that sticky feeling I always get when I fall asleep in the daytime.

"Go pour yourself some tea," I said. "I have to excuse myself for a minute." The downstairs bathroom didn't have a window, so I had to switch on the light to examine myself. I looked exactly like I'd just woken from a nap: rumpled hair, smudged makeup, sticky mouth. Yuck. I cleaned up, polished my glasses, and felt much more alert when I joined Robin in the kitchen. Angel had come in, and the two were in conversation about Angel's previous movie experiences and Robin's loathing of Hollywood.

"I thought you loved it out there," I said, surprised.

"I did at first," he admitted. "I liked being somebody to people I thought were important. I liked being a noteworthy person. Writers don't get that too much, even in Hollywood, where you'd think they'd be revered. Those beautiful faces have to have words to say, after all. When I first arrived out there, I had a desirable property—my unfinished book—that several studios wanted. At first a really famous actress had an option on it. She wanted to play you." He grimaced, an expression I really couldn't interpret. "But then she went into rehab, and the option lapsed, and enthusiasm was cooling. The book actually came out, hit the best-seller list for a month, and interest built back up. A studio optioned it for one of its up-and-coming boy actors. They were going to beef up the role of Phillip."

Phillip, my half-brother, had been staying with me when the murderer was arrested.

"Go on," I said.

Robin looked weary, but he did offer me a little smile. "Then the boy wonder backed out because he got a chance to do the new musical version of *Treasure Island,* and he wanted some stage credentials. In the meantime, the book went off the best-seller list, naturally. So, after all the hills and valleys, this production company optioned it for a made-for-cable miniseries, and hired Celia for it a few months before she won the Emmy."

"Was that when you met her?"

"Yes," he said, and wiped a big hand across his eyes. "That was when I met her."

"I'm sorry," Angel said. I nodded.

"Like I said," Robin told us, visibly pulling himself together, "it was really over. There was a lot to admire in Celia, a lot of talent, but she also had a full measure of the selfishness actresses sometimes have. And there was definitely something going on with her these past few weeks."

"Someone coming," Angel said.

Then I heard the crunch of the gravel as a car made its way up the driveway.

Arthur was here, as he'd said earlier. I sighed. I just couldn't help it. I wondered how Lynn, his ex, was doing, raising their little girl. I'd heard Arthur took the child every chance he got, but still...

By the time Arthur knocked on the front door, Angel was making some coffee and I'd put some cookies on a plate. It was my attempt to soften the edges of an official visit. It didn't work, of course. Arthur was glad of the coffee, turned down a cookie with a pat of his waistline to explain the refusal, and got immediately down to business.

Angel and I went over our morning in detail, including approximate times and whom we'd seen and when we'd seen them. Arthur was particularly interested in my account of who I'd noticed at Celia's trailer door, but I pointed out that I hadn't been watching every second, and I'd only observed the door for maybe ten minutes. You had to figure that the murder had happened after Will, Mark, and the unknown woman (Arthur thought she must be a sort of sub-assistant director named Sarah Feathers) had spoken to Celia. That would have been while Angel and I were talking to Carolina.

"That Tracy girl who works for Molly's Moveable

Feasts had as good a view of the door as I did, and for far longer," I said.

"Yeah, but her attention was constantly distracted by people coming up and wanting juice, coffee, a pastry, to pass the time of day…"

I nodded. I could believe that.

Arthur wrote everything down and asked me and Angel a million questions. Robin sat silently and listened. Just when I thought we must be through, he said, "Do you live out here alone, Roe?"

"Yes."

"Do you think that's a good idea?"

I could feel my eyebrows draw together in a frown. "If I weren't comfortable with it, I wouldn't do it, Arthur," I said, in a final tone.

Because I'm short, some people think I'm helpless, or feeble, or silly. Arthur had known me for years; Arthur had even told me he loved me on more than one occasion. Why he would love a woman who would live in a place that terrified her when she had adequate means to move, I don't know, but he had that little smile that made me nuts. Patronizing.

"Do you really think you're safe out here?" he asked, trying ever so hard to sound gentle.

"Hell, Arthur, I've got a security system that's hooked up to the police department switchboard!" I could feel my face getting hot. Arthur had an amazing ability to make me angry. I was not about to tell him that this very day I had made up my mind to move.

"Okay, okay!" He held up a hand, palm outward, placatingly. "But for a woman alone, living in town is safer."

Much more of this, and I'd feel the steam coming out of my ears. "If you've gotten all you need from Angel and me…" I said, making sure there was a nudge in my voice.

"I ought to be going, too," Robin said. "They may need me back at the motel. I'm sure Joel is having a meeting this afternoon to decide what to do."

"I have to pick up Joan at the sitter's," Angel said apologetically. "Roe, would you like to come back to town with me? Spend the evening?"

There was no way in hell I was going to admit I wanted to be with someone, not while Arthur was standing there looking sorry for me. "I have a lot to catch up on here," I said, keeping my face calm as a pond. "Thanks for visiting, Robin. I'll talk to you later, Angel. Tell me when you need me to take you to pick up your car." Angel patted me on the shoulder. She'd asked Robin for a ride back into town, and he'd seemed glad to oblige. If I'd been him, I wouldn't have been too enthusiastic about getting back to the motel to face Joel Park Brooks, either.

To my dismay, somehow Arthur managed to linger while Angel and Robin left.

"How is Lorna?" I asked brightly, fishing the little girl's name out of my memory with a desperate yank.

"She's great," Arthur said, his eyes focused on my face. Not too many people look at you so directly, but Arthur had always been a forceful and direct man. Except when he'd been dating me, and sleeping with Lynn Liggett. And asking her to marry him, when she was pregnant. Except for that. "She's in the first grade."

"Oh gosh," I said, the impact of the years that had gone by hitting me between the eyes. I remembered how jealous Martin had been of Arthur, when he found Arthur pursuing me after Arthur divorced Lynn. All that emotional energy, wasted.

"Yes, I know." Arthur laughed a little. "They've moved into Atlanta. Lynn wanted to put Lorna into a private school, so she took a job with a big company that installs security systems for businesses. She's pulling in the big bucks."

"How often do you manage to see Lorna?" I was struggling to keep the conversation going.

"I have her two weekends a month," Arthur said. "And some holidays."

"Did you remarry?" I asked, all too aware that my voice was too bright and social.

"You know damn good and well I didn't," he said. He didn't sound angry—just as if he were dusting off my pretense of ignorance. "You would have known. I've dated a lot, come close to being that serious once."

I automatically wanted to know who the close call had been, but that wasn't something I could ask.

"How are you recovering?" he asked.

I bit my lower lip and looked down at the hardwood floor. "I'm probably doing better than I thought I would," I said.

"That sounds pretty uncertain."

I considered that. "I thought I'd really collapse," I said. "Then I thought I was just being brave for a while and I'd collapse after that. But I guess I won't ever."

"You seem surprised."

I nodded.

"He never was…" Arthur began, and I held up a warning hand. There was a long silence.

"I'm leaving," Arthur said. He rose wearily from the couch, ran a hand over his pale hair. 'Do you… would you like someone to stay out here at night with you?"

"You offering?" I was trying to get a little lightness into the conversation.

"I'd do it in a minute," he said flatly, and I was sorry I'd spoken.

"Thanks, but I'm used to being by myself at night." I did appreciate his thinking of my feelings. But the habit of turning Arthur away had gotten so strong I couldn't break it, and it would really be bad for me to begin asking someone to spend the night at the house to keep me company—not to mention what it'd do to my reputation, though I was pleased to find that consideration was strictly secondary.

"If you need me, you call," Arthur said. "But I know I make you rattled." He looked resigned to that. "There's someone who'd love to stay out here with you, and she needs money, if a paying situation would be more comfortable for you. The new young patrolwoman is just panting to meet you. She'd be glad to keep you company, especially if there was money involved."

"Oh, she's on the poor side?" Why on earth would anyone want to meet me? Oh...the movie. Someday, I'd quit being completely naïve.

"Her husband ran up all their credit cards as high as he could before he left," Arthur said, carefully showing no expression.

"He ran off with someone?"

"Her stepbrother."

I let that soak in for a minute, until I was sure I had understood Arthur correctly. "I guess my own problems aren't too bad," I muttered, and Arthur nodded.

"That does put your life in perspective," he agreed. "Plus, the SOB took their car."

"That's one of the worst stories I've ever heard," I said after I'd thought it over.

"Tell me about it. So, if you want Susan to stay with you, give me a call." Arthur patted me on the shoulder, walked across the front porch, and opened the screen door. "And call me if you think of anything about this morning, or about last night. Anything that might have happened while you were having dinner with the movie people."

"I will," I said, feeling sure I'd already told Arthur everything that could have a bearing on the murder of Celia Shaw.

I stood in the living room, all alone, and looked at

the clock on the table. Amazingly, it was only noon. Equally amazingly, I was due at work.

Breakfast (two pieces of toast) had been an eon ago. I got some chicken salad out of the refrigerator and ate it out of the bowl, with crackers to scoop it up. I was glad I had a job where I was due, glad something had broken into the dreary pattern of my life...

Where had *that* come from?

I wasn't glad Celia was dead, was I?

No, not really. I was just glad something had happened to change things, jolt me out of my misery, cause people to treat me as something other than pitiful.

Because I wasn't, I told myself crisply. I was not pitiful, and I was not just a forlorn rich widow. I was no tragic figure to be wrapped in cotton batting, either. I was a *kick-butt* rich widow. I began to feel better and better as I cleared away the cracker crumbs and the glass, and by the time I got in my car to go back to town, I was in a mood to take on a grizzly.

No one looking at my four-eleven exterior could tell I was loaded for bear, and it was a considerable surprise to Lillian and Perry when I told Janie Finstermeyer that her son had way too many overdue books, that it was getting to be a real habit of his, and that she'd better energize him into getting to the library with those books before the day was over or we'd yank his card.

I turned away from the telephone to find them staring at me as if I'd dyed my hair green.

"Can we even do that?" Lillian asked.

"You just watch me." But it wasn't necessary to put the threat to the test, because Josh Finstermeyer flew into the library as if propelled within an hour, money in hand and an apology on his lips. He even took his baseball cap off in the library.

I tried to be equally gracious.

Eight

Of course, I heard from my mother that night. My mother, tall and elegant and reminiscent of Lauren Bacall at her coolest, might as well have been born on a different planet from me; I cannot imagine her carrying me in her womb, no matter what evidence there is to the contrary. I am an only child, and I've seen pictures of her pregnant, so I guess I'm really hers.

I was never much a child of my father, except biologically. He left when I was in my teens, my early teens. My mother, in her excellent vengeance, became a real estate tycoon in a modest way—if a tycoon can be modest—and lived in more affluence than I ever would have if I'd stayed with my newspaperman father. He'd remarried, and had a son named Phillip, my half-brother. I hadn't seen Phillip in years. My father had decided I reminded the boy of a traumatic incident, and that seeing me was bad for Phillip.

When he got his own computer, Phillip began email-
ing me. I could tell, in his first messages, Phillip considered himself daring, contacting his dangerous older
sister. I replied so calmly and matter-of-factly that it
made my teeth ache, but at the same time I tried to
make it clear that I was very happy to hear from him.
Now we exchanged news once or twice a week. I hadn't
had much to tell him since Martin died (Phillip had
sent me the biggest, most sentimental card he could
find, covered with a glittery substance). That wasn't the
case tonight.

When the phone rang I was busy trying to tell Phillip
about the excitement of the movie shoot, without
dwelling on the death of Celia Shaw. Seeing the movie
set and the movie people through different eyes made
me feel better about the whole thing, myself.

I picked up the phone absently, my mind still on my
composition.

"I hear you met up with Arthur Smith today," my
mother said.

"It's the first time I'd seen him in years," I said. "He
looked pretty much the same."

"Not dating anyone now," my mother informed me,
and I didn't ask her why she'd bothered to find that out.
She wasn't giving me information about an opportunity,
she was warning me. She'd never forgiven Arthur for
dating Lynn while he was dating me, and especially for
getting Lynn pregnant while I should have been.
Mother's slacked off on the grandkid issue since she has

some stepgrandchildren through her husband, John Queensland. Especially once I told her that I had a malformation of the womb, and it was very unlikely that I would ever be able to have a baby: I'd tried to keep that to myself as long as I could.

But even if I told her I was dying to present her with a grandchild, she wouldn't want Arthur to be the father—not any more. In her opinion, he'd publicly humiliated me. (Actually, that was true. But I had given up minding.)

"So, that poor girl who died was the one who was going to play you in the movie?"

"Yeah, the composite me. Weird feeling."

"Do you know Robin Crusoe is here?"

"Yes, I've seen him."

"How does he look?"

"Much the same. He dresses better. His hair's still red."

"Are you coming to dinner tomorrow night?"

"Oh…oh, sure." I rolled my eyes at the computer screen. The last thing I wanted was to go to a family dinner with all John's kids, their spouses, and the children. But I'd agreed a few days ago, guilted out because I'd skipped the last two such gatherings.

"I'll see you tomorrow night, then, at six. Please don't be late. You can bring someone if you want."

She always said that.

"I won't be late," I said firmly. I never was: Roe Teagarden, punctual librarian. Didn't I sound exciting? I sighed after we'd said good-bye, pretty much standard ritual after a phone conversation with Aida Teagarden Queensland.

But my mother had always done her best by me, and she loved me. I loved her too. It would have been nice if I hadn't had to constantly remind myself of that. Abruptly, I was fed up with my own whininess, and decided it was high time I went to bed.

This had certainly been a highly eventful Saturday, compared with my normal weekend routine. I suppressed the memory of Celia's appearance when she was dead, and instead spun myself a fantasy in which Joel Park Brooks came to my door and begged me to take her place in the movie, and I did so with completely unexpected talent and grace, and some incredibly attractive actor—not anybody obvious like George Clooney or Mel Gibson, but someone more cerebral, like John Cusack—came to my door and begged me to return to Hollywood with him and tan by his pool and be his love goddess, since I was far more genuine and original than the shallow movie beauties surrounding him…

There's no age limit or personality conflict in fantasies, and this one merged pleasantly into sleep.

Next morning was a good Sunday for church. I attend on most Sundays, but sometimes I'm more enthusiastic than others. I wasn't sure what was happening to me, what process had been set in motion this past week, but I was relieved to feel better. I didn't realize how long a dark cloud had hung around me until it began to lift. I slicked my hair back and put it up as smoothly as I manage, and I wore a fall suit of a russet color. I put on my gold-rimmed glasses, and I had suede pumps and a purse to match. Amber earrings, I decided, and a dab of perfume.

"You look good," I told my mirror earnestly. "Pretty *darn* good."

I got to St. Stephen's about nine-fifteen. We had an early service, since Aubrey also preached at another church about thirty miles away at eleven o'clock. I slipped into the pew I usually used, noticed my mother and John hadn't gotten there yet, and slid to my knees to pray. Our church is small and beautiful, and just breathing the air of it makes me feel better. The organist began her playing before I'd finished, and I eased back into the pew and listened with my eyes closed. I don't have much of an ear for music, but I thought I was listening to Handel. The pew creaked as someone sat by me, and I opened my eyes after listening a little longer. Robin was on his knees next to me, wearing a perfectly proper suit and tie. He sat back by me, and began the business of book-marking his hymnal and turning to the proper place in the Book of Common Prayer. When he was arranged to his satisfaction, one of his long, slender hands reached over and patted mine. I turned my hand palm up so he could clasp it, and he gave my fingers a squeeze. His untidy hair was freshly washed and floating around his head in a coppery nimbus, and I averted my face so he couldn't see me smile.

Robin released my hand with another pat, and the processional began. We stood to observe it, and bowed at the passage of the cross. I was reminded all over again of how much taller he was than I. As Aubrey, the lector, and the two acolytes disposed themselves at the front of the church, I saw Will Weir, the cameraman, scuttle into the back pew on the other side. He was wearing a sports jacket, a white shirt, and jeans; not standard churchgoing garb in Lawrenceton, but he was a visitor, after all. My mother and her husband had slipped in late, as well.

The sun poured in the windows of the church and I watched dust motes dance in the beams. The ritual unfolded exactly as it ought, and as the congregation knelt and stood in unison, I felt a deep calm wash over me.

Will scuttled out of the church as fast as he'd scuttled in, so he apparently didn't want to meet and greet. Astonishingly, Robin went through the whole ritual. I gave him every opportunity to detach himself from me, because I was naturally aware that there was going to be speculation. But with the greatest tenacity, Robin stuck to my side and walked me to my car.

"My mother wonders if you'd like to come to dinner tonight," I heard myself saying. Actually, that was true. She'd yanked me aside and ordered me to extend the invitation.

"How would you feel about that?"

I looked up at his small hazel eyes, fringed with rusty lashes. I looked down at my feet. "If you'd like to come, that would be fine, of course."

"Come by and pick me up at the hotel?"

"All right. Five-thirty okay?"

"Sure. Casual dress?"

"Oh, yes. I'll go home and change to pants and a shirt."

"Will you let your hair down?"

"I don't know. I hadn't thought about it," I said, more than a little surprised. I started to ask him why he wanted to know, but reined myself in. I also felt an impulse to ask him if he wanted to come home with me for lunch, and zapped that idea, too. Instead, I gave Robin a small smile and wave, and got in my car to go back to the house.

What an interesting morning it had turned out to be.

Arthur was parked in my driveway when I got back.

"I like the hair," he called.

I sorted through my keys and nodded in reply as I went to the side door. "Come on in," I called, unlocking the door and deactivating the alarm.

Arthur was wearing a suit, and he was clean-shaven, but I was fairly sure he hadn't been at church.

"You're dressed up," I said tentatively.

"I was on the news." He looked embarrassed. "You wouldn't believe how many news people are down at the station."

"I haven't been watching the television. I guess it was everywhere on the news." Arthur nodded. I was standing in the middle of my kitchen, tucking my keys back into my purse, and thinking as hard as I could. "Oh, this is bad. They'll be coming around again."

"Soon as they get directions to your house."

I said a very unladylike word.

Arthur laughed. "You can say that again. You know if it gets bad you can come stay with me."

"I think not," I said, smiling. "Notorious Widow in Cop's Love Shack?"

Arthur took a deep breath. "Listen, Roe, who in that movie crew was especially close to Celia Shaw?"

"Almost anyone would know more about that than I know." I slung the purse onto the counter, slid out of my pumps, and made some fresh coffee. I got a mug out of the cabinet and put it by the coffeepot, and I got out some sugar and milk for Arthur's coffee. Funny, if you'd asked me how he took it, I wouldn't have thought I remembered—but here I was, setting out the things he took.

"I have reasons for asking you."

"I'm sure you do. Well, of course, Robin dated her…though there were signs that the relationship was over."

"Like her going to bed with your stepson?"

"Yeah, like that. No, really, there were indications before that."

"Who else?"

"She seemed to be big buddies with Meredith Askew. I'm not sure how two-way that was, but Celia used Meredith to deliver her messages."

"What about other crew members?"

"Will Weir was with her when I ran into them while they were shopping."

Arthur consulted his notes. "He would be the head cameraman. I understand he's more famous in his field that Celia Shaw had gotten to be in hers."

"Well, he has a few years on her."

"Anyone else?"

"When we went out to dinner at Heavenly Barbecue, Mark Chesney went."

"He the assistant director? The gay one?"

"Right. Well, that is, he's the assistant director. I don't know about the gay part." Actually, that was a conclusion I'd reached myself. I found that I was unwillingly impressed. There was no telling how many people Arthur had interviewed yesterday. He was definitely on top of this investigation.

"Did you notice anything peculiar about this actress?"

"Peculiar? How so? Mentally?" I'd seldom seen anyone more focused than Celia Shaw.

"Physically."

"Yes, I had noticed some things. She stumbled a lot," I said.

"Stumbled." Arthur looked...not exactly excited, but intent.

"Yes, she was a little clumsy on her feet. And once she slapped at the director and looked surprised, like she didn't know she was going to do it."

Arthur looked down at his feet. He didn't want me to see his face.

"So, are you going to explain?" I am as curious as the next person, and this was truly aggravating of Arthur.

"It'll be in the papers," he said, more to himself than to me. He looked up. "No, I just can't. We're trying to keep it quiet as long as we can."

He had done this on purpose, I figured, to punish me for my lack of interest in him.

"Of course," said Arthur, his hard blue eyes fixed on my face, "if you were to butter up the lead detective sufficiently…"

"Define 'butter up,'" I said, my voice tart. I hoped he didn't mean what I thought he meant.

"A cup of that coffee would be nice."

I flushed, and poured him the coffee. It smelled so good, I decided I'd have more, too.

"You didn't open your paper this morning."

"No, I save the big Sunday paper for the afternoons."

Arthur slipped off the rubber band and unrolled the paper. Celia's murder was the below-the-fold story on the front page. I blinked at the amount of coverage. The picture of Celia was one taken at the Emmys, when she'd been hanging on Robin's arm. She looked fabulous, and very young. Robin looked awfully mature, compared to Celia.

I motioned at a chair at the table, and Arthur sat. I slid into the chair across from him and began reading. The more I read the hotter my cheeks got. There were several references to the age difference between Robin and Celia. There were several references to Barrett. You didn't have to be Miss Marple to read between the lines.

When I'd finished, I couldn't look up at Arthur. This

time it was I who didn't want him to read my face. I was wondering who was responsible for the slant of the story. Was it this individual reporter? Was this the way Arthur had read the situation, and had the facts he'd released to the papers been selected because they followed Arthur's reading? Or had this reporter been talking to Barrett?

I was willing to bet on some combination of all these elements. There were details about the evening at Heavenly Barbecue that had "Barrett" stamped all over them, especially the inclusion of my name. It could easily have been left out of the story, and my presence at that awful meal clearly had no bearing on Celia's death—or at least, none that I could fathom. Barrett wanted to cause me discomfort and inconvenience, and he had.

The phone rang while I was thinking, and before I could answer it, Arthur picked it up. I felt rage prickle at the backs of my eyes while I waited for him to hand over my own telephone to me.

"Sure, she's right here," Arthur was saying, and as he gave me the receiver he got a good look at my face. I don't think he'd quite realized that he was upsetting me, but he sure knew now.

"Roe?" It was Robin.

"Yes."

"Have you…are you too busy to talk?"

"No, not at all."

"You sound kind of funny."

"I'm in a mood," I said, with self-control.

"Yes, I can tell. With me?"

"Oh, no."

"Have you read the paper?"

"Yes. It was just brought to my attention."

"Do you...are we still on for tonight?"

"Definitely."

"Good." He sounded flatteringly relieved. "This may be hard to arrange, because I'm besieged here at the motel."

"Let me think. I'll call you back."

He gave me his room number, which he'd forgotten to do at the church, and I said good-bye. I hung up and swung around to face Arthur.

"Don't answer the telephone in my home."

"I apologize. I was out of line. It was a reflex. I should have thought."

"Now, I need you to go. I have things I have to do this afternoon." I wondered what I would do if Arthur wouldn't leave, but I pushed that thought down into a corner as hard as I could. It wouldn't do to sound the least uncertain.

"All right," he said. "I'm sorry to have bothered you." Now he was getting all stiff and huffy. Screw it. No more Ms. Nice Widow.

I stared at him, unrelenting, until he stuffed his pad back into his pocket and stomped out. I set the alarm behind him. I watched from the window as he drove away. Again, I felt the isolation of this house. It was definitely time to move.

I wondered, as I turned away from the window, what big secret he had been going to tell me. I was proud of myself for not softening, but at the same time it was irritating to be left hanging that way.

As Robin and I had eventually arranged, I picked up a key at the desk and then pulled around to the back of the motel about two hours before my mother's dinner. We'd allowed plenty of time in case something went wrong.

Though they weren't in the front, where the office was, there were lots of reporters camped out in the side parking lot of the motel, and some television news vans. It had been easy for them to find out where the movie crew was staying. The men and women of the media were milling around on the pavement. Some of them had brought deck chairs, and some of them were playing cards.

I shook my head. I would not make a living as a reporter for any amount of money. No one could pay me enough to sit in a motel parking lot just in case someone should stick his head out of a door long enough to be photographed or interviewed.

I still had my hair up and I was wearing dark glasses, a rudimentary camouflage move. I scooted up the stairs to a room on the second floor, not even glancing out over the railing to see if I was being observed. I had noticed Shelby's car parked two slots down, and that was one big relief. Shelby had rented the room I'd just entered under his own name, and left the key at the desk for me.

I called up to Robin's room. Shelby answered.

"He's ready," Shelby said when he recognized my voice. He sounded amused.

"Okay. The door's unlocked."

Shelby hung up; he was a man of few words.

In less than two minutes, the door swung open, and Robin walked in dressed in Shelby's blue padded Pan-Am Agra winter jumpsuit. It was what the men out in the plant wore when the temperatures dropped. Shelby was not as tall as Robin, but he was wider, and the poor fit was not so noticeable. The day was just barely cool enough to make the heavy garment reasonable.

"Can I take it off, now?" Robin asked. "It's cutting me in a, uh, tender area."

"Sure, take it off till it's time for us to leave," I said, trying not to smile too broadly. I hadn't figured that Shelby's suit would be too short in the crotch for a long man like Robin. I perched on the end of the bed to watch.

"I see that smile," Robin said, his voice muffled by his attempts to take off the jumpsuit while he faced away from me.

His nice clothes were somewhat rumpled by the experience, and his hair was disheveled, but he emerged from the heavy jumpsuit looking relieved. "I'll put it back on before we go. You're sure your friend doesn't mind doing this?"

"Not as long as he gets his jumpsuit back. I owe them two hours babysitting now."

"That doesn't seem too bad. I'll help."

"You won't be around," I said. "You'll be back in Hollywood."

"No. I don't think so."

He sat beside me on the end of the bed, and what you might call a significant silence fell. I was scared to look up at him, but eventually I just had to.

But I couldn't ask him what he meant.

He kissed me.

I can't say it was totally unexpected, but it was still a sort of shock. I hadn't kissed anyone since Martin died. And I hadn't kissed Robin, of course, in many years. But there was a familiarity to it, a kind of renewal, instead of the shock of something new.

Maybe because we were in a motel room, and I didn't have anything of my former life around me, maybe because I had that pleasant zingy feeling that I'd put one over on a lot of people with my plan to sneak Robin out for an innocent dinner at my mother's, maybe just because I hadn't had sex in a hell of a long time, but I went up in flames. It was all I could do to keep from grabbing him and throwing him to the bed. This was not my usual style. I was trembling with the effort of suppressing my reaction to his mouth.

"Roe?" he said, almost whispering.

He had put his hands on either side of my face.

"A little more," I said.

"Aren't we a little mature to be making out?"

"You want to go sit on that chair over there?"

"Oh, hell, no."

"Then mind."

"Let's lie down as our next step," he suggested.

"Okay." I scooted up on the bed after kicking off my shoes, and Robin did the same.

"It's a lot easier to kiss you when we're lying down," he observed, after a minute or two.

"I had noticed that."

"Let's do that some more."

So we did. It was like being teenagers again. We were thoroughly frustrated when I called a halt to the proceedings. But I just couldn't take that step. I just wasn't quite ready. Though God knows, my body was.

Robin vanished into the bathroom, and reappeared a few minutes later, looking more relaxed. He wedged back into the jumpsuit. My blouse was buttoned and tucked, and I'd put on my shoes.

"Is your mother just as formidable as she was a few years ago?" he asked, watching me brush my hair, which I'd taken down. With a little help. I carefully pinned it in a knot.

"She's softer around the edges. Marriage and having grandchildren by way of John's kids has really fulfilled her." I was still enjoying the pleasant sense of having been naughty.

"Remind me to take you to a motel room more often," Robin said as we trotted down the stairs and scrambled into my car. No one called out to us. The jumpsuit and the hairstyle evidently were enough camouflage. "If we'd stayed a little longer, maybe I

could have had my wicked way with you." He had
jammed a baseball cap over his telltale red hair, and
I turned my face away to hide my smile. Every man
I knew wore a cap at some time or another and
looked quite natural, but not Robin. He looked like
an ostrich dressed up for Halloween. I was relieved
when he pulled it off when we got into downtown
Lawrenceton.

The scene at my mother's house was chaotic. John's
two sons and their wives and their children made the
two-story four-bedroom seem positively tight. I had always liked John: warming up to his sons Avery and John
David had taken a little longer. They'd been a little
wary of my mother and me, too. The fact that John and
my mother had signed a prenuptial agreement that was
very clear on who got what when they passed away had
been a great help, and my mother's cordiality and courtesy had won over her new stepdaughters-in-law.

Melinda, Avery's wife, was braiding her toddler's hair
in the foyer when I stepped in. Her infant, Charles, was
in one of those portable carriers, which was on the floor
where she could keep an eye on him. Charles was awake
and watching his mother and sister with wide eyes.

"Hold still, Marcy!" Melinda was saying, her tem-
per obviously at the breaking point. Marcy, of course,
picked the entrance of a stranger (Robin) to spring into
her worst behavior. "No!" she shrieked. "It hurts! Daddy
do it! Daddy do it!"

"No, your daddy's busy. I'm going to braid your

hair," Melinda said firmly. My respect for her mounted. I would have gone searching for Daddy instantly.

"Melinda, this is my friend Robin," I said, when Melinda's hands had begun dividing Marcy's fine brown hair into three parts.

"Hi, Robin! I'd shake your hand, but I'm busy right now. I think your mom is in the den, Roe." Melinda's fingers flew, braiding like hell while Marcy was standing still.

"Hey, Aunt Roe," Marcy said, looking up at us. She eyed Robin. He must have seemed huge to her.

We located my mother in the den, as Melinda had said. She was serving glasses of wine, but she put the tray down so Robin could give her a small hug (nicely calibrated on Robin's part). Then there was a round of handshaking among the men. John had recovered from his heart attack, but he was thinner and didn't move as quickly as before. He was still a handsome man, and he'd passed his looks to Avery and John David, tall brown-haired men with blue eyes. They were golfers like John, and they were both confident men who did well at their chosen careers. Other than those similarities, they were quite different, and their wives weren't anything like each other.

Avery, Melinda's husband, was an accountant. Avery was very traditional, and people who weren't also completely buttoned down were somewhat suspect in his book. He'd never been really sure about me. Melinda herself, though pleasant, was none too bright. But she seemed to have this raising kids thing down pat, and she was active in community work.

John David, the younger brother, had been a wild child. There was still a gleam in his eyes that said he was anticipating the unexpected. His wife, Poppy, had also made a name for herself as a teenager, but now she seemed quite settled into her role as a suburban wife and mother. She still enjoyed an evening out every now and then, and I would not have put money on either of them maintaining fidelity during their marriage, but I liked both of them quite a bit. Their new son, Brandon Chase Queensland, was the most placid baby I had ever encountered.

As I might have predicted, Avery questioned Robin cautiously about his means of making a living, his future plans, and his upbringing. John David wanted to hear stories of the famous people Robin knew, and instantly treated Robin as if he was my acknowledged companion.

"Not too surprising, since you have a hickey on your neck," my mother murmured into my ear, and I jumped a mile.

"Oh, hell," I said, clapping a hand over the spot she touched with one cool finger.

"Everyone's already seen it," she said with a shrug. "You and Robin seem to have picked up where you left off." My mother's graying brown hair was beautifully styled, as always, and her tailored blouse and gray slacks were as informal as she got.

I took her arm and we stepped into the dining room, which so far was empty of Queenslands.

"The only thing is," I said, with the frankness you can only show your family, "I think about Martin and I just feel so guilty."

My mother took a deep breath. Her eyes looked old, suddenly. "You listen to me right now, Roe. Your husband is *beyond* all that."

I sucked in my breath.

"Martin—yes, while he was here he truly loved you—but Martin has *passed beyond* those emotions that plague living people—jealousy, possessiveness, selfishness. He's not here, he doesn't worry about worldly things any more, and he should not affect your decisions."

I was silent—mostly from the shock of her frankness—as I pondered my mother's pronouncements. "You're sure you believe this," I said, half-asking a question. "Because you know…Martin, as he was, would rather have killed Robin, and maybe me, too…."

"And that wasn't Martin's best side," my mother said calmly. "But these things are no longer his concern."

That idea caused a painful ache. It detached my life even further from Martin's. And yet, I could not deny that I felt a lightening of my heart, as if the fact that it was still emotionally tied to Martin's had been dragging it down.

"You are the best mother I've ever had," I said, and my voice came out shaky. She laughed, and I laughed, and I gave her a hug, and then she went back to her company. "Melinda, have you got that girl's hair braided?" I heard her asking as she went into the living room.

A mumble from Melinda, then Marcy's voice, shrill and piercing, "Is that big man with Aunt Roe a giant?"

The whole house seemed to hold its breath for a second before laughter came from at least three different rooms.

Nine

"She had Huntington's chorea," Sally Allison said. This was big news, and Sally relished big news.

It was eight in the morning, and I'd just finished getting dressed for work when the phone rang. Sally had called to ask me the same questions Arthur had asked me the day before: had I noticed Celia Shaw exhibit any of a list of symptoms?

"Yes, yes, yes," I had answered. I detailed once again what I had observed. "Now, what does that mean?"

When Sally told me, I was just as ignorant. "What is that?"

"It's a disease, a horrible hereditary disease of the central nervous system," Sally said. She sounded almost awed by the horror of it.

I would have expected a certain amount of zest to Sally's words; after all, reporting on the horrible was her bread and butter. But whatever Huntington's chorea was, Sally truly thought it was awful.

"So, what's the bottom line?"

"The bottom line is inevitable death with your mind reduced to vegetable status. You have no control over your body at all."

"Oh. Oh, gosh." That hardly seemed adequate, but then I didn't know what would.

"There can be lots of symptoms, and it can progress at different speeds in different individuals. Mostly, you begin showing signs in your thirties, and though it may lie almost still for a few years, it begins sinking its teeth into you."

"Oh, that poor girl." I wouldn't wish such an end on my worst enemy, and Celia had hardly been that.

"Well, actually, she was somewhat older than her official bio says," Sally told me.

"I kind of guessed that."

"Yeah, she was at least thirty. That's still young for Huntington's to have manifested itself, I gather, but it happens."

"Do you think she knew?"

There was a long silence.

"Maybe," Sally said. "Maybe she…I don't know. If she began wondering why she was getting so clumsy—I think she must have known something was wrong, if not exactly what."

"What about her mother?"

"That's it. I called the town where her mother died,

as listed in her bio, and though Linda Shaw committed suicide, fairly advanced Huntington's was found at the autopsy."

"Oh, my Lord. That's awful."

"But, we have to ask ourselves," Sally said wisely, "is her mother's death related to Celia's murder at all?"

"How could it not be?"

"It doesn't have to be."

I held the phone away from my face and stared at it. "Sally, are you serious? The mother has Huntington's and dies young, a suicide. The daughter has Huntington's, and dies young, an apparent murder victim. No connection?"

"You didn't realize she was ill. I don't know who did. Maybe the people around her all the time were well aware something was wrong with her—our old friend Robin Crusoe, for example. Wouldn't someone as smart as Robin Crusoe realize his girlfriend had some severe problems? Wouldn't her self-proclaimed best friend Meredith know? Wouldn't you at least suspect something was wrong if you saw me begin to make involuntary movements, begin to show unusual clumsiness? Maybe say something completely off the wall?"

"Yes," I said reluctantly. And you're not even my best friend, I added silently.

I just didn't want to believe that Robin had to have realized that something was up with the woman he'd been sleeping with. But I had to face the facts.

"I just don't see why anyone would kill her. So, she's

sick. It's not her fault, and it's not catching, am I right?"
I began doodling with a pencil on the pad I kept by the
phone in the kitchen. Robin had said he didn't think he
was going back to Hollywood. So where would he go?

"No, it's not contagious," Sally said, as if the very
idea was stupid. "It's hereditary."

"And it came through her mom. So, who's her dad?"

"No one knows. Linda Shaw didn't list anyone on
the birth certificate, but her sister, the one who raised
Celia, said Linda was not promiscuous, so she would
have known, presumably. And furthermore, the sister
says the guy was out in California with Linda when she
died, from what Linda would say when she called."

"So finding him would provide a lot of information."

"At least. Maybe he and Celia had been in touch,
who knows? She didn't talk about her family life to
anyone."

I could see why. A tough way to start your life, with
no dad and a doomed and distant mother: I couldn't
even imagine it.

"But what was the actual cause of Celia's death?" I
asked. "Surely someone killed her?"

"Oh, she was smothered with a pillow," Sally said,
almost as an afterthought. "After being drugged with
some tranquilizers, probably ground up in her coffee.
Maybe she was already unconscious when she was
smothered. Maybe she didn't even know. And then, a
little later, someone brained her with the Emmy. There
again, she didn't know."

But maybe she had, my morbid imagination insisted. To be too drowsy to defend yourself, to feel the pillow against your face, to want air so desperately…I shuddered, and tried to think of something else. A lot had been happening to Celia's body. "So she was dead when she was hit with the Emmy?" I asked, just to hear it again.

"Yes. She was killed three different ways. The pills, the smothering, the statue."

"That was sure a quick autopsy."

"Since there's so much media interest, she got moved to the head of the class," Sally said cheerfully.

I found this all too depressing. I was just beginning to take a lighter look at my life, and I could not bear to be pulled down. I'd woken up looking forward to the day ahead—a mindset I'd once taken for granted—and I was selfish enough to want to hold on to the feeling. I had brushed my hair back in a ponytail, then rolled it up into a ball and pinned it, topping the whole with a bow low on my neck. I was wearing rust-colored pants and a light sweater, tan with rust-and-green patterns on it. My tortoiseshell glasses coordinated. Before Sally had called, I had been feeling a distinct glow.

It was difficult to believe that my whole balloon of happiness had been inflated by the simple fact that I'd given a man an erection. But when I tracked my new attitude down to its source, this was what I found. Well, what the hey. I'd settle. It wasn't the erection per se. It was the fact that I still *had it*. Okay, granted, to excite the human male was fairly easy (sometimes just the state of breathing was enough). But Robin had standards above that, I told myself stoutly. He'd had a high-powered agent, he'd had women in Hollywood (where beautiful women were a dime a dozen), and still, yours truly had excited him. I had a suspicion that if I examined my line of reasoning I would find many flaws, but that wasn't the kind of mood I was in.

I was determined not to brood on Celia Shaw's terrible end. I told myself briskly that Arthur was on the case and he was a good detective, and I should leave it at that. I took another rotation in front of the mirror, deciding that my bottom looked real good in these pants. I dabbed on some perfume. I'd managed to cheer myself up to my former level by the time I breezed through the employees' entrance into the library, slung my purse into my little locker and pocketed the key, and collected my usual pile of memos and mailings from my pigeonhole in Patricia Bledsoe's office.

She looked up from her computer, gave me a brisk nod, and returned to her work. I nodded right back, and began flipping through the medley of garbage that was my daily tree consumption. Lying between memos from the regional director about how many hours of course work were required to keep one's library degree current, and the seasonal reminder detailing the symptoms of head lice, was a plain dime-store envelope (in these days, you should call it a plain Wal-Mart envelope, I guess) with a folded sheet inside. I never got personal mail at the library. Only my name was written on the outside, in neat block capitals.

"Patricia, who brought this in?" I asked, holding it up so she could get a look at it.

"I don't know. It was on the floor by the checkout desk this morning, Perry said. He brought it back here," Patricia said. She didn't seem too interested. As usual, she was ironed, starched, aligned, and every other straight-and-narrow adjective I could recall.

"Well, hmph," I said. I put everything else down and borrowed Patricia's letter opener, which seemed to irritate the woman. Tough. I tapped the letter out of the envelope; a plain sheet of five-by-eight white lined paper, torn from a tablet.

It said, "You Whore she's not even buried and your after her boyfriend."

I stared at it as if it were a poisonous snake. I wanted it to go away, or to say anything other than what it actually said. I took a deep breath and tried to think what to do next. An almost irresistible impulse seized me, told me to rip the paper to shreds and burn those shreds. I didn't want to admit to myself that someone had directed words so venomous to me, much less admit to anyone else that I had received such a message. But Duty is practically my middle name—well, maybe Conventional, or Law-abiding—anyway, I had to call the police.

Of course, the cop who answered the call was Arthur Smith.

* * *

He held the paper with a pair of tweezers as he read it. His face remained blank. "This is very interesting," Arthur said, in a voice that would've sounded genuinely detached if I hadn't known him so well. He asked Patricia the same questions I had about the letter's provenance, plus about twenty more, all designed to elicit any detail she might have omitted.

It was interesting to watch Arthur with Patricia. She answered his questions clearly and in detail, but she never looked directly at him, and she didn't elaborate. It was like she was counting out the words she had to use to get her message delivered, and that was the number she would utter—that many, and no more. To my alert eyes, Patricia looked absolutely relieved when Arthur drew me from her little office into the employee lounge, which was deserted.

"You've been with the writer with the stupid name?" he asked.

He knew quite well who Robin was.

"Depends on what you mean by 'been with,'" I replied. "If you're talking biblical, that's none of your business. But my mother asked him over to dinner last night, and we had to sneak him out of the motel so the reporters wouldn't follow. So, yes, I've spent time with him. I've known him for years." It was remarkable how defensive I sounded for someone without a guilty conscience.

"Who knew this?" Arthur was nothing if not tenacious.

"Any of the movie people at the hotel, I guess," I said

slowly, thinking as I spoke. "My family—my mother and John's family, that is. And Shelby helped me get Robin out of the motel, so Shelby and Angel knew." I detailed the little plot to Arthur. It all sounded silly today, though yesterday it had seemed to make perfect sense.

"A lot of people," Arthur said. He looked at the letter again, frowning. "I don't want to alarm you, Roe, but you should do some thinking. The last woman who dated Robin Crusoe got smothered. Now you've gotten a nasty letter."

I was flabbergasted. "There's a great distinction between being killed and getting an anonymous letter," I said, trying to sound tart and undaunted. But I was turning over what he'd told me, and I was dismayed; and that was what Arthur had wanted, for whatever reason.

"What was the name of the secretary?" he asked me, out of the blue.

"The lady you just met? Patricia Bledsoe," I said.

"Is she new to Lawrenceton?"

"Comparatively. She's lived here maybe a year."

"She have family?" he asked idly.

"She's got a son, Jerome. He's in the fifth or sixth grade, I think."

Arthur stared at the wall of her office as if it would open to reveal Patricia Bledsoe. He shook his head as though whatever he was trying to recall just wouldn't pop into his head, a feeling with which I was all too familiar.

"Where's she from?" he asked, as if he were losing interest.

"She never talks about herself." That was a remarkable thing all by itself. "I only know from seeing her application that she moved here from Savannah."

"Savannah. Okay, let me get this back to the station, send it off to the crime lab. You get any other mail like this, you call me right away. You did the right thing." He sounded a little surprised.

"Yes, I know," I said, taken aback by all this unnecessary chatter. This wasn't like Arthur.

"I'd stay away from Robin Crusoe," he threw over his shoulder, which was far more Arthur-esque. Suddenly, he turned around, marched over to me with purpose in every step, and kissed me. I could not have been more surprised if he'd unzipped his pants. Stunned and unhappy, but anxious not to hurt Arthur's feelings—we'd hurt each other enough over the years—I endured the pressure of his lips, my hands hanging limp at my sides.

Then it was over, and he stepped back, giving me a baffled, angry look that I didn't know how to interpret. He walked out without looking back.

Arthur was like a dog with a favorite old bone, I decided as I wiped my mouth and set my mind in the right mode for work. He couldn't quite forget about it, and he couldn't quite abandon it. He kept digging it up and chewing on it, then putting it back in the ground.

That was where our long-ago affair should stay; dead and buried.

* * *

Mondays are always iffy at the library. Some Mondays are just dead; people are running errands and shopping and picking their work week back up after the weekend. But then, we have regulars who finish their library books on the weekend and come in Monday for a new supply. Teachers are fond of assigning term papers on Monday, and there are kids who come in to check out all the available books on a certain subject so they'll be sure of a resource.

This Monday was one of the quiet ones. Of course. I really wanted to be busy, to take my mind off the confusing events of the past week, but the most exciting thing that happened was catching a twelve-year-old girl trying to sneak out a copy of a new magazine that featured a cover article about her favorite boy band. I caught her on the way out the door, explained her options to her, and gave her a Kleenex when she started crying. Josh Finstermeyer of the overdue books saw me standing with the weeping girl, and hid behind the stacks to see if I'd stick bamboo under her fingernails. He clearly regarded me as the devil incarnate. I had to confess, it sort of gave me a thrill to be considered so formidable.

Tracy, the young woman from Molly's Moveable Feasts, came in. She waved to me while giving me a brilliant smile, and settled in a chair to read some newspapers. I guessed nothing was happening at the movie set yet.

About ten minutes before five o'clock, Robin loped through the glass doors. His long legs ate up yards of carpet like nobody's business. His hair was more of a mess than usual, and he was wearing khakis, a sharply pressed shirt obviously fresh from the laundry, and an old corduroy jacket. All he needed was a pipe clenched between his teeth, or maybe a golden retriever on a leash.

I was shelving books and, after he located me, he followed me as I trundled the little cart.

"When do you get off today?" he asked in a low, library voice. He pressed his hand against my back at my waist and left it there, while I put a Lauren Henderson book back on the shelf. His hand felt very warm. After a second or two, *I* began to feel a little warm.

"At five," I said, glad to hear my voice come out cool and controlled.

The next book on the cart was Linda Howard's, and she was on the top shelf. I stretched up as far as I could and still could not quite slide Ms. Howard into the right slot. Robin stepped closer to help, and after the book was in place, he stayed right behind me...in fact, so right behind me that he was sort of nudging me.

"Robin," I said, a little question in my voice. Spooned, that was what we were. My curves... his—oh.

"Mmmm?"

"The book is where it's supposed to be."

"And?"

"You should move."

He sighed. "If I must," he said, and stepped back a little.

I smiled at the books in front of me. "I assume you had a purpose in coming to the library?" I resumed rolling the cart. I may have headed down a deserted row. In fact, there was nothing to shelve at all in this area.

"I heard there was a *very* strict librarian here," he said innocently.

I half-turned to give him a look, my eyes wide. This was a whole new ball game, one I'd never played. Hmmm.

"Oh, yes, very strict," I said, trying to sound calm and assured. I wasn't sure where this was going, but I found myself quite interested in finding out.

"One who might punish me severely for having an overdue book," Robin said.

"Have you been talking to Josh Finstermeyer?" I blurted.

Robin looked disconcerted. "Who's he?" he asked.

"That boy in the corner who's trying to hide behind the shelves."

Robin looked as if he was having trouble suppressing a laugh. "Robbing the cradle, are we?"

I sighed. "Can we get back on track here?"

"I don't know; if Josh Finstermeyer is your beverage of choice…"

"Robin!" I growled. I felt that everyone in the library was watching us, and I was right. Perry was taking a gander, as was young Josh, to say nothing of Tracy, who'd lowered her newspaper to stare. I felt my face turning red.

"I have two overdue books," Robin said, his face suddenly serious. His voice was soft and significant. I looked up at him. "Two," he emphasized. He waggled his eyebrows.

"That's...*very* bad." I narrowed my eyes. For the first time in my life, I wished I had a riding crop. I would flick it against my boot.

He bent down to my ear. "I turned down the corners of some of the pages," he whispered.

"You do need to be punished. At length," I said. I raised my eyebrows to make sure he'd get it. "At *length*," I repeated.

He was a little pink himself.

"Maybe you should come to my room tonight," he said, very low. "To collect my fine."

I decided to escalate.

"Why not now?" I said coolly. I glanced at the clock. "I'm off work." I gave him a challenging look.

His eyes widened behind his glasses. He ran a hand through his hair, which looked as if he'd been doing that all day.

"Can you hold this mood on the drive out to the motel?" he whispered in my ear. Very close.

"It's entirely possible." My house was a lot closer, but I knew without considering the idea closely that my house was out. I cast a blessing at him for not suggesting it.

"Then let's go."

"I'll go clock out."

"You remember my room number?"

"Yes."

"I'll be waiting for you."

"You'd better be," I said, in my stern librarian persona.

"Ooooh," he breathed, giving me a look that let me know for sure he was into this.

I clocked out and retrieved my purse in record time, and was getting into my car in the employee parking lot behind the library when I saw Tracy approaching. Oh, heck, no! I was in a mood, and I didn't want to get out.

I decided if I were behaving uncharacteristically, I'd just go all the way. I pretended I didn't see her and pulled out of the parking lot when she was just a few feet away.

I had other fish to fry.

Robin, probably as uncertain as I was, was still fully dressed when I knocked on his door. But he had lit some candles and drawn the curtains tight.

"On your back, miscreant," I said sternly. I had always wanted to say "miscreant."

There was delight in the crooked smile, quickly smothered by a very well assumed expression of fear. "It was just two books," he pled, stepping out of his shoes and socks and lying on his back on the bed. Yep, he was excited, all right.

"That's two books too many," I told him. "You have to learn your lesson." With an expression of severity, I began unbuttoning my blouse. "What's the worst punishment you can think of, you…scofflaw?"

Robin winced, and I could tell I would pay for that one, later. "The worst punishment," he said thoughtfully. "The worst punishment would be to have to perform sexually, again and again—with only the briefest breaks for naps and food—for a small naked woman with…" His eyes widened. I'd taken off my bra. "Oh, boy," he breathed.

I climbed on the bed and straddled him. As I looked down at him, his eyes darkened. I took his glasses off and put them by mine on the bedside table. "Can you think of anything that would make that punishment worse?" I murmured, bending down to him. My lips were an inch from his. My hair fell around his face.

"I would be forced to make you come twice for every one time I do," he said, his voice rough and deep.

"Then I guess you better get started."

Ten

I was changing my clothes when the phone rang. Almost without looking at my caller ID, I was sure my mother was on the other end of the line.

"Where were you last night?" she said, considerably agitated.

"I spent the night with a friend," I said with commendable restraint. "Now I have about fifteen minutes to get to work."

"A friend? Who?"

I let the silence hang.

"Oh," she said slowly. "That kind of friend."

More silence.

"Oh, sorry. Well, that's just...I didn't mean to intrude. I just wanted to make sure you're okay." I could practically hear the questions seething over the line. I was proud of Mother's self-control.

"I'm fine, thank you." In fact, more than fine. I was relaxed and mellow to an extent I could hardly believe. Except for the discomfort when I walked. Or sat. Or crouched.

I picked through my sweaters, looking for a turtleneck. Surely it was cool enough to make a turtleneck not unreasonable? I glanced into the full-length mirror on the closet door. Definitely needed the turtleneck. "Oh, Mom, I need to look for a house in town and put this one on the market."

Quite a silence on the other end. "Aren't you rushing into this?"

"I'm not rushing. I had already decided to move back into town." The last thing in the world I needed today was to have to defend myself to my mother.

There may have been a little edge in my tone, because she immediately said she'd list the house that very day. "Who would you like to be your realtor?" she asked, keeping her voice scrupulously neutral. I'd had Eileen Norris the last time I'd been house hunting, but I had a better idea this morning.

"Why, the head honcho, of course."

"Really? You think we can gee and haw together?"

"Sure. After all, this is your area of expertise."

"Well, tell me what you want, and I'll line some things up."

"I have no idea." I tried not to wonder if Robin really meant to stick around in Lawrenceton, if he planned to buy a house or rent, should I be thinking

of getting a house that would hold another person—
and his books. No, no point in thinking of that. Jumping the gun, for sure. "I guess I want a three-bedroom,
but I need a room for a library, and a dining room, and
a living room. And you know how I feel about plenty
of kitchen counter space. On the other hand, I don't
want much yard to take care of."

"Your house is ready to show, I'll bet," Mother said.

"Yes. Isn't that scary? All I'd have to do is pick up the
floor of my closet."

"I'll list it today," she promised. "I hope this is the
start of a new era for you, honey."

"I guess it is," I said, after turning that over in my
mind. "I think it is." We discussed the price I should set
on my house and what I was willing to spend on my next
one. I was once again grateful for my financial health. The
independence it afforded me was absolutely blissful.

"What's your work schedule like the rest of the
week?" my mother asked.

"I work this morning, but I'm free this afternoon."

"Let me see what I can line up by then."

"Wow. So quickly?"

"I didn't get where I am by letting my feet drag,"
she said.

"Okay. I'll come by Select when I get off work."

"Good, I'll see you then."

The movie crew had resumed its activity at the courthouse this morning. I could tell from the traffic snarls

in the area. Robin had said they would be shooting the scenes that didn't include Celia's character, until the re-casting of the role was accomplished. He didn't expect that to take long.

I glimpsed the Molly's Moveable Feasts van parked a block away from the courthouse, and saw the familiar table set up further down the street. A man was in charge of it today. I wondered where Tracy had gone, and what she had wanted with me the day before. I could feel my cheeks burn as I thought of what had followed the little scene in the library. Just when you think you know yourself...well, it had been the most fun I'd had in a long, long year.

"Patricia," I said, trying not to sound disgustingly cheerful. "How are you today?" She was taking the cover off her computer and making little preliminary movements of things on her desk. Her pencil had to be just so, her little magnetic bowl of paper clips in a specific location, her chair exactly the right height.

"Just fine, thank you, Ms. Teagarden," Patricia said in a clipped voice. "What do you think the police are up to, with Celia Shaw's death?"

"I have no idea. I haven't talked to anyone in the police department since the day it happened."

She looked disappointed. "Oh," she said. "I understood you were a particular friend of Detective Smith's."

"No, that's not correct." I could do clipped, too. "As far as I know, they could be coming to arrest you any minute."

My mildly belligerent comment had an amazing result. Patricia Bledsoe stared at me as though I'd grown a second head. She turned absolutely green.

"What do you mean?" she said, her voice faltering.

"I was just, ah, emphasizing how little I know about the investigation," I said, convinced I'd gone over a line somehow. I felt knee-high to a grasshopper. "Patricia! You, of all people...I mean, I bet you iron your *underwear*."

Patricia looked at me with loathing. "Go work," she said.

She'd crossed the boundary into open rudeness in a great rush. What on earth had I done? I felt pretty truculent myself, by now. I couldn't think of anything to say that wouldn't escalate the hostility in the room, so I spun on my heel and left, my excellent mood stuffed in a sack for at least a little while.

My boss, Sam Clerrick, came in the employee door as I was stuffing my purse into my little locker.

"Good morning, Roe," he said. His heavy glasses reflected the overhead light. He was carrying his briefcase, which was as much a part of Sam as his white shirt and tie. You'd think he carried nuclear warhead firing codes in it instead of library paperwork.

"Watch out for Patricia today," I said.

"Something's wrong with Patricia?" Sam was as protective of his prize secretary as if she'd been a pedigreed bitch.

"She's a mite testy," I said, trying not to sound spiteful.

"Have you gone and upset her?" Sam sounded calm,

but I knew better. A good secretary, one who meshes perfectly with her boss's moods and personality, is worth rubies. Sam would much rather see me quit than lose Patricia.

"She went and upset herself," I said in my own defense.

"You obviously didn't know that the day Celia Shaw came in here and checked out some books, I gave Ms. Shaw a brief tour of the library," Sam said.

Oh, I bet that had just made Celia's day. "I'm sure she enjoyed it," I muttered.

"And she met Patricia then, shook hands with her," Sam went on. "So naturally Patricia is upset by the news of Ms. Shaw's murder."

"I see that I shouldn't have brought it up," I said, and that was the truth.

Casting me a hostile look, Sam stomped into Patricia's cubicle. I could see him saying soothing things through the clear upper panels.

So much for senior employee loyalty, I told myself, now just as frazzled as Patricia. I'd been working for the library for ten years or more, and Patricia had been here less than a year.

I stomped out to the main desk, emotionally loaded for bear. Luckily for my coworkers, about ten minutes after the library opened, the heavier of the two ladies who worked at Flower Fantasies brought in a beautiful flower arrangement and carefully set it on the desk in front of me, as I was beginning to telephone the people who had overdue books. Chrysanthemums, daisies, and other flowers I couldn't identify mixed in a medley of warm colors against their dark green background.

"It's for me?" How long had it been since anyone had sent me flowers?

"Yes, ma'am," the woman said, beaming at my pleasure. "First order of the day."

I took the card out of the little plastic prongs and opened the envelope.

"You are beyond beautiful," the card said. It was signed "Robin."

I didn't melt on the spot, but it was a near thing. Tears welled in my eyes, which I kept very wide open.

"It's lovely," I said. "Thank you."

"Enjoy," she said, waving a casual hand, and returned to her van, parked illegally outside the main library doors.

I held the card to my chest like a schoolgirl, while I beamed at the arrangement. If Robin had planned a blitz attack on my body and heart, he was going about it exactly right. I could only be glad he'd decided to proceed with his campaign.

After the freezing-cold misery of the last year, I had the feeling I was sitting by a warm fire. That glow lasted all morning, with the exception of the few minutes it took to roust a reporter who came into the library to ask me how it felt to have been murdered by proxy, so to speak. Sam took care of him pretty quickly, and I was grateful.

The incident did set me to thinking back to that

morning at the courthouse. I recalled sitting in the sun, waiting for Angel. I watched Will speak to Celia, shove the door shut with one hand while he carried a cup of coffee in the other. I watched Mark knock at the door in vain. Had Celia been angry with him? Had she already had the drugged coffee, begun feeling drowsy? Had she just been in the bathroom and unable to come to the door? Then the woman—Sarah Feathers, Arthur had told me—just barely opening the trailer door and speaking a few words, shutting it again. Then I'd lost a few minutes of surveillance while I talked to Carolina. Then I'd gone to Tracy's table in front of the Molly's van, watched her change jackets, had the orange juice. All trivial stuff.

I opened my eyes and focused on my flowers again. I'd been standing there with my eyes shut while I thought, probably a bad habit to get into. For the first time, I wondered if Sarah Feathers had heard a reply from Celia to whatever she had said. I didn't know Sarah Feathers, and I couldn't ask her, but I knew who could.

Sure enough, Angel had gotten Carolina's cell phone number.

"Hello!" Carolina said, after two rings. I asked my question, and she said, "I don't know why you want to know, but it's easy enough to find out. I see Sarah all the time."

Carolina agreed to call me back that evening. I went back to calling patrons about overdue books.

At noon, I trotted out of the employee door with my

flowers held carefully in front of me. I was so busy planning how to place them in my car so they didn't fall over that I never saw the shadow behind me until it was too late.

"Roe! Roe! Are you all right?" A silhouette was between me and the bright fall sun, right overhead.

"What happened?" I asked, my voice weak and shaky.

"Someone ran up behind you and hit you," Perry Allison said. "Someone in a coat with the hood pulled over his head, so I couldn't see who it was. I called the police on my cell phone. They're coming."

"My flowers," I said, and I began to cry. That was why I felt wet. My flowers were all around me on the pavement of the parking lot, and the water in the vase had soaked my pants.

"I'm sorry," Perry said. "Are you hurt?"

"I'm okay," I said, trying to convince myself. A patrol car was turning into the library parking lot already, and a patrol officer I didn't know leaped out of it as though the car had an ejector seat. She was a small woman with short, dark hair, and she was already talking over her shoulder-rig thing.

"Which way did the assailant go?" she asked Perry.

Perry, trying not to gawk (he is a big fan of authoritative women) pointed in the direction of the heavily planted slope that divided the parking lot from the lower street. "He went in the bushes after he pushed Roe down," Perry called to the officer's back.

"Wow," Perry said, deeply impressed.

I sighed, glad I wasn't one of those self-centered people who think getting attacked is all about them. This was my day for people ruining "Aurora" moments.

Perry looked back down at me, maybe hearing something exasperated in my exhalation. "Can you sit up, Roe?" he asked. He slid an arm underneath me and I was upright. I'd never been this close to Perry before, and it felt funny. I would just as soon he let me handle this on my own, but there was no way I could say "back off" without sounding incredibly rude.

"This is good," I said, more or less to myself. My head felt fine. After a second or two of thinking about it and getting my breath back, I decided I wasn't really hurt, just astonished.

The patrol officer came back through the bushes. "I'm afraid the assailant has escaped," she said seriously. "There are other officers patrolling the area right now." I wondered if she always talked like that, or if she'd acquired the habit since she joined the force.

"I'd like to stand up if you would give me a hand," I said, giving Perry my right hand and extending my left to her.

"You sure you're okay for that?" she asked. "Did you hit your head?"

"No, I took a spill when she shoved me," I said.

"She? This man," she inclined her head toward Perry, "said your attacker was a 'he.'"

"Why did I say that?" I asked myself, while they

pulled me to my feet. I thought it over. "Perfume," I said.

"The person who pushed you had on a woman's fragrance?"

"Yes, officer," I said. "But I didn't see her coming at all. She just ran up behind and pushed me down and I dropped my flowers." Embarrassingly, I began crying again.

"Who were they from, Roe?" Perry asked, probably hoping I'd stop with the waterworks.

"Robin," I sobbed.

"Way to go," he said. "I'm Perry Allison," he added to the patrolwoman.

"Uh-huh. Susan Crawford."

"Pleasure to meet you."

"How you doing, Miss?"

"Thank you, I'm okay." I was still drizzling tears, but physically I felt all right. "I'm Aurora Teagarden."

"You *are?*" Now she was fully engaged. I looked up into her face, and realized that Patrol Officer Susan Crawford must be the young woman Arthur had told me about, the new officer whose husband had left her. "I've wanted to meet you for ages," she said. "I'm sorry it's under these circumstances."

She pulled off her dark glasses, and I saw her eyes were clear and gray. She wasn't wearing a speck of makeup, and she looked just fine. "Thanks for coming so quickly," I said, not really sure how to proceed. "What do we do now?"

"I'll write up a report," she said. "Mr. Allison, how was the assailant clothed?"

"What?" he asked, as if he'd been jogged out of a daydream. "Well, this man—or woman—was wearing a hunter green coat with a zipper in the front and one of those hoods you can drawstring shut right around your face. He had on gloves and gray sweat pants, I think."

"Thank you. Is this your place of employment?"

"Yes, ma'am," Perry said. "Any time you need me, I'm right here."

"I'll bear that in mind." She wrote a few lines in a notebook, talked into her radio, and then began to look around the parking lot, which was not very large to start with. Perry and I began picking up the scattered remnants of my arrangement, and I began inwardly gathering myself back together. After all, the flowers could be rearranged. My clothes needed changing, that was all. I wasn't even hurt to any appreciable extent; bruises and scrapes only.

The attack had been malicious rather than harmful.

I half-expected Arthur to show up. Any time anything had happened to me in the past few years, he'd been there immediately. A police detective has no great problem keeping tabs on someone. But Arthur was a no-show, and I was really relieved. Sally walked down from the newspaper office (she had a scanner on, full-time) and took the incident as casually as I could have hoped.

I left in my car after I'd talked to the humorless Officer Crawford again. I stopped by the florist, where I explained I'd dropped the arrangement, and could she be an angel and reconstruct it? At my cost, of course.

She would be an angel, she agreed. And within the hour.

I ran out to my house and changed, searching out my only other turtleneck. Luckily, it was cream colored and I could wear it with anything. Anything, today, turned out to be forest green pants. I pitched the soiled clothes into the washer. This was no time to abandon my ultraclean habits, considering my mother had left a message on my answering machine to tell me she'd be showing my house at three in the afternoon.

Quick work, even for Mother.

My face was bruised, as I discovered when I went to the mirror to brush my hair. Apparently I hadn't quite been able to stop myself from banging the pavement. Well, my hands had been full, and I hadn't thrown them up in time. It could have been much worse. What if my attacker had had a knife?

A thought skittered across my mind, and returned to take a deeper look out of my eyes.

Robin's last girlfriend was lying on a slab in Atlanta.

Robin's current girlfriend—and I guess that would be me—had just been shoved down in a public parking lot in broad daylight.

The two incidents weren't exactly comparable, were they? Still…food for thought.

Robin called the library before I got off work to ask if he could come out to the house. I appreciated him not assuming he could show up, and I said I'd be glad to see him. Which was true. But I would've been more glad if I could've seen him somewhere else.

I was still uneasy at having another man out to the house I'd shared with Martin. Surely that was natural? And I could tell my mother was debating whether I was moving because of Robin's reappearance in Lawrenceton. That would be nuts, I knew. Robin said he wasn't leaving town when the movie shoot was finished, but men said a lot of things under the sway of lust. My experience with Arthur had taught me nothing, if not that.

I wasn't moving because of Robin, I assured myself. I was moving because I was ready to rejoin life. And if that life included Robin right now, so much the better.

I was carrying the arrangement when I got out of my car, and he came over to me to help.

"They're beautiful," I said. "Thank you so much."

A little awkward, he bent to kiss me, his hands full with the bowl of flowers. The minute his lips met mine, I felt a sort of solar flare. It was unexpected and violent, and I thought the damn flowers would end up on the ground again.

When we broke for air, I took a deep breath.

"This seems, I don't know, a little precipitous," I said.

Robin's eyes were shut behind his glasses. He was breathing raggedly.

"Feels good, though," he said.

"You're coming off a relationship and a loss, I'm coming off a relationship and a loss," I pointed out. My relationship, and my loss, had been far greater, but he knew that already. We walked over to the house.

"What happened to your face?" Robin said. It was dark already, and I'd just disarmed the security and flicked on the kitchen lights.

"Does it look very bad? I've been dodging mirrors since noon," I said. My fingers anxiously patted the darkened area. I trotted to the downstairs bathroom, Robin at my heels. I leaned across the sink, my glasses folded on the counter, and peered at my right cheek. Not too bad—a dark center and a lighter ring of bruising. It would be gone in a week.

"You want to tell me what happened?" Robin asked.

It crossed my mind that Robin had not expected me to call him about this. He was waiting for me to tell him—not angry at not knowing already. This was a different reaction from the one to which I'd grown accustomed. Robin definitely approached life differently from Martin, and his expectations were different, too. I shook my head at myself. I should not compare.

"You don't want to tell me?" His voice sounded mildly teasing, nothing more. But I could tell from the way he stood that he was more serious, now.

"Someone ran up behind me in the library parking lot and pushed me down. The flowers were in my hands, and I couldn't drop them fast enough—I didn't *want* to drop them—so I kind of hit the pavement hard."

"Someone attacked you?" Robin was quite rightly astonished. "In the library parking lot?"

"Yeah. Strange, huh? Right out in daylight."

"The police didn't catch him?"

"Or her. No, the police didn't."

"Why 'her'?" Robin's face was involved in thought, suddenly. I could practically see the lightbulb over his head.

"I thought I smelled perfume." I eyed him. "Does this ring some kind of bell with you?"

Robin looked profoundly embarrassed. "Ah, maybe." He did everything but look up at the ceiling and whistle. "But I…maybe if I went and talked to her….I hate to say anything unless I'm sure."

"That's what people in mysteries say right before they get killed. 'Yes, I think I know the killer, but I have to check a few things before I talk to the police.' Next scene, they're toast."

Robin was struck by this observation, which as a mystery writer should have occurred to him first. "That's true," he murmured. We'd drifted from the bathroom into the kitchen, and I'd gotten out a pitcher of tea. He nodded when I lifted it, a question on my face.

"Okay, well. This is really…there's this girl. She…" Robin turned a dark red. He took a big swallow of tea. "She has this big thing about me. Like a superfan. She took this job to be…" Robin was overwhelmed with chagrin, shook his head speechlessly. Hollywood had not made him completely egocentric, I thought, smiling at him.

"She's nuts about you?" I suggested.

He nodded morosely. "You know how I found out about Celia and Barrett spending the night together? I knew already when I came to the trailer. I got an anonymous note. I'm about ninety percent sure it was from her."

I began to put two and two together, myself. "Tracy," I said. "Tracy, from the Molly's Moveable Feasts catering company."

"Yep." Robin finished his tea in one long gulp.

I thought this over. "Did you tell the police about Tracy?" I asked.

"No," he said, horror written all over his face. "This isn't exactly something I want to talk about, Roe."

"Robin, didn't you consider the fact that the woman murdered was your girlfriend?"

"Former," he corrected. He looked at me almost angrily. "Of course, Roe. What are you…?" His face cleared. "Oh."

I saw the tide of realization pour over him. "Oh, no," he said. "Oh, no."

"I hope not," I told him. "But you have to say something."

He fumed and fussed, but he was just postponing the inevitable. "You think she may have attacked you today, too?" he asked, as he pulled his coat back on to drive to the police station.

I shrugged. I remembered Tracy's face, after (I now realized) she had seen Robin and me together in the library, obviously close, obviously in lust. I wondered what would have happened if I hadn't pulled out of the parking lot, if I'd waited to talk to her as she'd wanted. I was really glad I hadn't stopped to find out.

Eleven

I met my mother in front of a house on Oak Street. How perfect could that be? Every town has an Oak Street. Hearts of oak, the Old Oaken Bucket, Tie a Yellow Ribbon Round the Old Oak Tree.

The street name would have been perfect. The house wasn't. The living room was an awkward rectangle, the bathrooms tiny and inconvenient.

As I might have anticipated, my mother was less than patient with my quibbles. If she'd been more of a stranger, she'd have had to listen quietly. As it was, she argued—until I commented that I could easily switch realtors. "In fact," I said, "I could go to Russell & Dietrich. They'd laugh all the way to the closing." After that, Mother seemed to understand that if I said I just didn't like the house, it wouldn't do to quarrel with that feeling.

So our first evening out, we came up with zip. Mother had lined up four houses to see; and I had objections to all of them.

"The couple I showed your house to this afternoon seemed to like it," she said, before climbing into her new Cadillac. But by that time all I could think of was getting back to that house.

As I let myself in, I was shivering. The evening had cooled down very quickly, and I knew our warm weather was about to end for the season. As I tickled Madeleine behind the ears, I admitted to myself that our failure was actually a relief to me. If the house-hunting process had been too easy, I would have mistrusted it. It would take forever to sell this place, anyway.

I was sure of that until about eight o'clock the next morning, when Mother phoned to tell me that the people who'd seen my house the afternoon before had called her with an offer.

"What?" I gaped at the telephone.

"What can I say? They saw it, they liked it, they made an offer. It isn't even an insulting offer." It wasn't. It was actually a little more than I had been willing to settle for.

Suddenly, I felt as if the ground were falling out beneath my feet. I was terrified. I was losing my life.

"Roe?"

"Sorry. Just…having misgivings."

"You don't want to withdraw the house?" Mother was trying not to sound outraged.

"No. No," I said, trying to stiffen my spine. "No, I need to move. I just...when do we let them know?"

"You mean, you accept the offer?"

"I guess I do," I said, surprised to hear my voice saying the words. "I can't think of how not to. I just thought it would take months to sell this house. Months."

"Me, too," my mother said. "But this couple wants to live in the country. The house looks beautiful now. They have a son who loves to hunt. The man's father is coming to live with them, and he needs the apartment above the garage."

"Well. Counteroffer for two thousand more dollars," I said, hearing my voice as if it were coming out of someone else's mouth. "If they'll come up with that, I guess we've got a deal."

"There is one snag."

My heart gave a lurch of hope. "Oh?"

"They need it now."

"What?"

"They need the house as soon as you can get out of it. If that's before we can arrange a closing, they'll pay rent. It's a domino situation. They've sold their house, the grandfather has just retired and is driving down in a van full of his stuff, and they have nowhere to put him when he gets here."

"He can't just drive up and settle here in the yard."

"No, Roe, what I meant was that he can sleep on their couch, but that's going to be pretty unsatisfactory for more than a week or two."

"So, I need to find an empty house. And buy it."

"Or we need to work something else out. Of course, you can stay with me and John for as long as you need to, but I know you don't want to put your things into storage if you can help it."

We discussed the situation for a few more minutes, and Mother agreed to get together another lineup of houses to see that afternoon. I thought I'd calmed down, but I was still shaky when I hung up.

I thought of calling Robin.

No, I would not lean.

To my disgust, I began crying. I'd done fine on my own, just fine, until I'd met Martin and decided to marry him. Now, here I was, aching to have a man to talk to, used to having someone around to consult with, used to having a companion to share every little thing. I had missed that acutely over the past year.

The phone rang again. I was almost scared to answer it. But I did, since I am an optimist.

"Hey, this is Carolina," said her accentless California voice.

"How are you?"

"Busy as hell. I just wanted to let you know I did talk to Sarah, and she says she just opened the door, said, 'Thirty minutes till you're due on the set, Miss Shaw,' and shut the door again."

"No reply?"

"No, she didn't hear Celia say anything, and the light wasn't on in the trailer."

No, it wasn't until Barrett had opened the door wide enough to let in sunlight that he'd seen the body. I thanked Carolina and hung up.

The clock was telling me I'd be late for work. I finished yanking my clothes on, determined to go in to work as usual. I brushed my hair carefully, hoping its length and volume would obscure my bruised face and my hickeyed neck. As I hurried out to my car, unlocking it with a click of my keypad, it did cross my mind to wonder if I *had* managed so splendidly before I got married. Hadn't I always been looking? Hadn't I always longed to have someone to share my life with? Hadn't I always assumed I would find that person, sooner or later?

I had. And he'd violated the dream by dying on me.

I was back on a more or less even keel after I'd been at work for an hour.

Probably it was inevitable that I'd have emotional spasms of grief for some time to come, right? For the first time, I wondered if it would ever be over. Surely I'd grieved and raged enough. I'd waited almost a year to even look at another man. Granted, when I'd looked it had been more like an immersion, but I had not even thought about men until Robin reentered my life.

I was broody and worried about the house situation, but not tearful, when Robin called.

I seldom get calls at work, of course, and I was a little surprised to hear Robin's voice on the other end of the phone.

"Roe, hey, I'm back at the motel. Listen, are you free for lunch? I need to talk to you."

"Um, I guess so. Beef 'N More?"

"No." I could practically hear him shudder. "There's a pizza place on Kenneth Road. It used to be okay."

"Yeah, Trixie's. That would be all right. I get off work at twelve-thirty. Is that convenient?" It wasn't Robin's fault I'd spent the morning castigating myself for my longing to throw myself into his life.

"Sure. Is something wrong?" He didn't sound as though he really wanted to ask. I guess I hadn't been as successful as I'd hoped in keeping my voice neutral.

"I'm just fine," I said independently. "I'll see you then."

He might have sounded a little puzzled as he said good-bye, but that was okay.

As I was working the return desk, Mark Chesney came in. He was looking good today, wearing what seemed to be his work uniform of pressed blue jeans and an oxford-cloth shirt. He was carrying a small box.

"Aurora!" he said, looking as astonished to see me as I was to see him. "What are you doing here?"

"I work here," I said, trying not to sound too "duh." "You knew that, Mark. It's in the script."

"Sure," he said. "So, in real life, you really do..."

"Work in the library," I finished, trying to sound as matter-of-fact as possible.

"Okay," he said, still faintly stunned. "Here, ah, these are books that Celia had in her trailer. I guess she checked these out before we started shooting. And I brought some paperbacks that were lying around, in case the library can use them."

I glanced at the hardbacks, and then looked again. *The Seventies Bombers. Political Violence in the U.S. The Black Panthers.* And, sadly, *Diagnosing Your Own Illness.*

"She was doing research," I said, carefully balancing my voice between question and statement.

"Oh, yeah, remember? She talked about it while we were out at supper that night, I think. Her next project was a movie set in the late sixties, early seventies, about violence in the hippy era. She was playing a middle-class girl turned radical who builds a bomb in her basement with the help of an African-American friend. Based on a true story."

I nodded, as if I'd remembered all that. The truth was, I'd barely listened. I rummaged through the books. The paperbacks were an undistinguished batch of popular fiction, but we can always use books in good condition. "Thanks for bringing these in," I said. Mark turned his attention back to me. He'd been giving Perry the once-over. Perry hadn't noticed, for which I was grateful. Perry was not exactly Mr. Stable, and I couldn't ever gauge his reactions, even to more ordinary occurrences.

"Hope you get to come back to the set," Mark said politely. "We've got our new leading lady. She's flying in tonight, and we should resume shooting scenes with her tomorrow."

That must be why they'd gotten the trailer cleaned out so quickly. The new lead would need it. "Jumping into a part must be incredibly hard for an actor," I said, focusing on what he was telling me, rather than on my random thoughts. "How can anyone learn lines that fast?"

"That's the business," Mark said briskly. "She'll be studying on the plane."

"Not Meredith," I observed. He looked blank. "Meredith Askew didn't get the job."

"Oh, gosh, no. Meredith doesn't have the star quality Celia did. And that's what we need."

"Kind of hard on Meredith."

"That's the business, too," he said, shrugging. He smiled at Perry, who happened to be looking in his direction, and gave me a little wave before he left.

I picked up the medical book. A strip of paper had been inserted between the pages in the H's. Huntington's Chorea had been underlined. So the police knew, as I did now, that Celia had been aware of her problem. I wondered if she'd gone to a doctor when her symptoms had become obvious, or if she'd had some other kind of warning.

Poor thing. She'd known, and she had to have dreaded the disease's progress. But she should have been given the choice of how to deal with her death sentence. She should not have had that snatched away from her. Someone had drugged Celia, someone had smothered her, and someone had hit her in the head. She'd been killed so many ways. Had three different people wanted her to die? Or had one person caused so much damage? If so, why?

The plastic cover on *The Black Panthers* was torn, so I carried the whole box back to the repair area. That was a corner of the employees' lounge, the corner right by Patricia's cubicle. Nothing closed to view, here. We like to check up on each other, here at the Lawrenceton Library. The donated books would have to be processed back here, too.

After I'd placed the box on the table, I noticed that a thin manuscript was at the bottom. I fished it out. Mark had packed the script of the movie Celia had been signed up to shoot after *Whimsical Death*. I'd have to call him to ask if he would like to come by and retrieve it. I stuck it back in the box.

I examined our torn cover more closely. If Celia hadn't been dead, I would've had a sharp conversation with her about this book. She'd been underlining, though I admitted to myself I couldn't be sure that had been Celia. There were slips of paper stuck here and there through the pages. I flipped through, removing the slips. One had been inserted in the center of the volume, where there were pages of pictures. I glanced down at the Afros with that kind of superior amusement we give to past fads. I thought of showing some of the more outrageous ones to Patricia, as a kind of peace offering, and I looked over to her cubicle to see if she was overwhelmingly busy.

She was staring at me with the blankest face I'd ever seen. I couldn't tell if she was broadcasting fear, or anger, or just a feeling of stunned inevitability, but the emotion was strong and directed at me. Puzzled, I gave her a little wave like the one Mark Chesney had given me, and went back to weeding out the makeshift bookmarks. I risked a glance in Patricia's direction after a minute or two, and she was still sitting at her desk, but her head was bowed. I had never imagined Patricia looking defeated, or even cowed, but that was in her posture. I thought about going to speak to her. But since she was Patricia, and she didn't like me, and frankly I'd never particularly liked her, I just didn't.

The book looked like new, I thought proudly, after I'd finished replacing the cover. As I taped the last flap of plastic in place, Patricia walked by me, heels tapping on the linoleum, her trench coat belted around her tightly. She never looked in my direction. Her purse was hanging from her shoulder. She was talking rapidly into her cell phone.

"Please have him in the office by the time I get there. He's late for his orthodontist appointment," Patricia said precisely. Her eyes met mine as she pulled open the employee door and she registered nothing. I might as well have been invisible.

This was weird.

A second later Sam came out of his office, which opened into Patricia's. He looked at her desk and then he looked through the glass at me. He pointed at his secretary's empty chair and raised his hands, palms up, to ask a question.

I shrugged. I pointed to the back door and made walking motions with my fingers.

Looking unhappy and disturbed, Sam wandered back into his office. He left the door open, so he could see his paragon returning. Pale, fair, and losing hair at an alarming rate, Sam seemed an unlikely poster boy, but there was no doubt that he and Patricia had formed a mutual admiration society.

I was back at the return desk when I remembered an odd fact.

Patricia's son didn't have braces. In fact, Jerome was blessed with teeth so even and white I had remarked on them. So how come she was taking him to the orthodontist?

Robin was waiting for me at Trixie's. We ordered, and while we waited for our food I told him about my house situation. Somehow it didn't seem so dire after I'd told him, and I could feel myself begin to relax. When our pizza was in front of us, he carefully wriggled a piece onto his plate and said, "We need to talk about what the police told me this morning."

This wasn't a happy opening. "Okay," I said. "Shoot."

Tracy, it turned out, was on probation…in California. She'd just gotten out of jail for another stalking incident with another mystery writer, Carl Sonnheim. Her pursuit of him and her jealousy of his girlfriend had ended up with Carl in the hospital, his girlfriend on a plane to Canada to put some distance between her and Tracy, and Tracy in jail. While she'd been in jail, Tracy had trolled through the prison library and ended up with all of Robin's books. She'd transferred her attentions to Robin.

"Lucky you," I said.

"Right." He looked grim.

"So she came to Georgia, and got a job with Molly's? How'd she find out Molly was going to be the caterer?"

"She'd done catering work in the past and still had some professional connections. They didn't know about her troubles."

"Sheesh."

"Molly couldn't believe it, Arthur Smith kept telling me. Said Tracy was one of the best employees she'd ever had."

"Do they think Tracy killed Celia?" I had to ask.

"The drugs, the pillow…they say that doesn't sound like Tracy."

"The Emmy does?"

"Well, it's more in line with what she did to Carl. She's been spotted around town. They don't think she'll leave."

Now I felt cold all over. "Then why don't they grab her?"

"Various people have seen her, but none of those various people happen to have been cops."

"Oh."

"So…you're going to be careful, right?" He put his hand over mine.

"I'm thinking it's you who should be scared," I said.

"I'm thinking it's both of us."

* * *

On my way to rendezvous with my mother, I remembered that when I'd walked up to the catering table the morning of Celia's murder, Tracy had been changing into a fresh jacket.

What if the soiled jacket had had Celia's blood on it? I shuddered again, and found myself looking at everyone I passed, on foot or in vehicles, trying to spot a head of auburn hair.

But it's not my way to keep scaring myself. I didn't see Tracy, and I told myself that the odds were good I never would again.

I met my mother in front of a house on Andrews Street. This was a fancier house than the others I'd looked at, and the price reflected that. But it looked good from the curb, and I was feeling optimistic.

Thirty minutes later, I was disillusioned. How could people put so much emphasis on floor space in a bathroom, and so little on kitchen room? The master bath would have held a Third World family, while the kitchen existed to rotate around the microwave. However, it was a pretty house in other respects, and I needed a house in the worst way. I mentally short-listed this one.

The ranch on Swanson Street was beautifully decorated, but too small. Poky.

McBride Street was full of trees. Even in the October night, I could tell that both sides were lined with oaks. I'd known someone who lived here—who was it? One of my girlhood friends, I thought. When I got out on the sidewalk in front of the house, the memories poured over me. This had been her house! I couldn't quite recall her name, but it would pop into my head soon. I had always loved spending the night with her.

"Who owns this now?" I asked my mother.

"David and Laurie Martinez," she said, peering at the fact sheet in the light from the streetlight. "They got transferred to Colorado. So the house is empty."

"How much?"

Mother told me.

"Okay," I said, "That's not too scary."

Mother had unlocked the door while I hung back, trying to recall what had made the house so special.

We stepped into the entrance. It was floored with red tiles. The carpeted area to the left was the formal living room. The red tiles ran down the hall to culminate in the kitchen, a large room with an eat-in area. Along the hall were doors to a formal dining room, a bathroom, and two large closets.

The kitchen had just been updated with new cabinets and a new dishwasher. There was a large walk-in pantry. It lay open to a sizable family room with a fireplace. There were sliding glass doors to a patio. I was remembering as I looked. Debbie, the girl who'd lived here, had had an older brother who made my heart throb with adolescent passion. I smiled as I thought of his utter obliviousness to my adoration.

"Okay," I said again, sounding, to my own ears, cautiously positive. I didn't like the carpet in the family area, but that was easy to change. Not cheap, but easy. I pointed out its poor condition, and Mother nodded.

To the right, off the kitchen and family room, were three bedrooms. One was a huge master bedroom with its own bath, and the other two, somewhat smaller, bedrooms shared a bath.

Then—and this was the neat part—a hall ran from the kitchen further back into the property. There were cabinets on both sides of the hall, making it into an elongated storage area. At the end of the hall, with its own door, was an office lined with built-in bookcases. Debbie's dad had been an architect, and he'd done a lot of work at home. I didn't need a home office myself, but…I stood in the office door, suppressing every thought that popped into my head.

I looked at everything again. I looked at the huge windows in the master bedroom, wishing the house weren't in town. It would be necessary to keep the curtains drawn most of the time. Though I thought I remembered extensive planting outside the window—that would certainly help.

"Is there a fence?" I asked. Mother stepped to the light switch panel by the door of the bedroom, and began flicking. The outside lights came on. Yes, the backyard was fenced and the enclosed area included that outside the side master-bedroom windows. Yay!

"There's another couple who say they're going to

make an offer on this house after they sleep on it tonight," Mother warned. She sat on the window seat and reached up to smooth her hair. It must have been a full working day for her, but she looked, as always, smooth and composed.

"No, I think I'll take it now."

Mother's head snapped up as though I'd popped her with a rubber band.

"Let me see the utilities," I said, holding out my hand. She put the fact sheet into it somewhat dazedly.

The electric bills were a little high. I wondered how long it had been since someone had blown insulation into the attic. "Where's the attic access?" I asked, and Mother told me it was out in the garage. We trailed out to the garage, to the west side of the house, which more or less faced south. The room was just a big old bare garage with the usual oil stains and battered cabinets, but it did have a door that raised and lowered. "Is the attic floored?" I asked, and Mother had to confess she didn't know. I let down the attic access steps and mounted. There were planks over about a third of the available area.

"Who are the next-door neighbors?" Back on the ground, I dusted off my hands on my pants.

"Ah, the Cohens on one side; they're retired, they have grandchildren. On the other side the Herman sisters. They're in their forties. Both widows. I forget their married names."

Sounded quiet.

I really liked the house and its layout. The square footage was comparable to the house I had now; a little less, but I didn't need any more. This house was in a good part of town, and I would have no trouble selling it if it didn't suit. I loved the red tile floors, and the redecorating would be minimal. The paint in almost every room looked as though it had just been redone.

"I'll take it."

Mother said, "It's not a coat, Roe."

"I believe I understand that."

She sighed. "You're right. You're a smart girl, and you know what you want. You always have."

Haven't always been able to *get* it, I told myself.

Mother pulled out her cell phone, consulted a list from her purse, and punched in some number. "David? Hi, good evening. This is Aida Queensland."

Mother listened. "Yes, I do have some good news. I have a client who's made an offer." She looked at me with one eyebrow raised. I tapped the selling price with my finger, then held up three fingers. I pointed down with my thumb.

"Three thousand less than the asking price," Mother said into the phone. "She said she'd need to replace the carpet in the family room." Pause.

"I can always counteroffer," Mother said next.

I wondered how many people had owned the house between Debbie's family and the Martinezes. I wondered where Debbie was now. Mother was doing some more listening.

"She doesn't have to wait for a loan," Mother said. "In case you think later that I was being devious, I have to tell you that the buyer is my daughter, Aurora Teagarden. She plans to pay for the house directly.

"Yes, I know, she's lucky to have that much available cash.

"Yes, it'll take a few days to get the paperwork done. But with no loan to apply for...I'll FedEx the agreement to you.

"Okay, we have a deal."

Those were my favorite words.

She hung up and nodded.

I took a deep breath.

Well, there was nothing like jumping off a cliff. In fact, I'd gotten a running start.

Twelve

Robin called Thursday morning, while I was lying in bed trying not to be terrified at the magnitude of what I'd just done.

"What are you doing this morning?" he asked. "I called the library and they said you weren't scheduled to work this morning."

"No, I go in this afternoon and work this evening. I'm just lying here trying to make a list of what I need to do. I bought a house last night."

"You what?" He sounded as though he thought he'd misheard me.

I explained.

"Wow. I just called to see how you were feeling after being knocked down in the parking lot. I didn't expect to find out you were changing your life."

"Yet again. Oh, I have a bruise on my face, and my

knees are a little sore, but I think I'm going to live," I said, scaling my news to a more expectable level. "Have you heard from the police again?"

"No more sightings," he said. "That's good. That Detective Smith, he can hardly stop asking me questions. Um, I'm not trying to imply anything, but was he formerly some significant male to you?"

"That's a nice way to put it. Yes, he was, briefly. Until he got another detective pregnant and invited me to the wedding."

"Ouch. Painful."

"It was, at the time. I'm over it." Though I was beginning to wonder if Arthur Smith ever would be; his continued emotional absorption with me seemed strange, since I'd been the injured party in our little triangle. Of course, I hadn't known I'd been in a triangle. Oblivious me.

"When do I get to see the new house?"

"Right now, if you want. I need to go make a list, have a look in the daylight."

"Give me the address."

Forty-five minutes later, I was walking up my new sidewalk, carrying two cups of coffee I'd picked up at the drive-through of one of Lawrenceton's fast-food places. I had some cholesterol-packed sausage biscuits in a bag. Luckily, Robin pulled up right behind me, and was able to take the bags while I unlocked the front door. My mother had given me the key, not without a sharp look or two, since she really wasn't supposed to be doing this. The privileges of being a realtor's daughter are few and far between.

Robin looked around curiously while I put our breakfast on the counter.

"How come you're not at the set?" I asked.

"They don't want me," he said casually. "The new actress is having her first morning of shooting, and she's pretty nervous. Actually, they never want me to be there, but they have to put up with me, from time to time."

"Then why did you come to Lawrenceton at all?"

He swung around to face me. His hair was as much of a mess as usual, and his glasses sat on his face crookedly. His cheeks were as smooth as a baby's bottom, and he smelled good.

His silence made me move restlessly. "What?"

"I came because of you."

I didn't know what to say. I didn't know how I felt.

"I wanted to see you again. I wanted to see if I really felt so comfortable with you, or if I was remembering it as better than it was. I had never slept with you; I hadn't seen you in years. You'd been married. What if it had all been something I made up when I couldn't find anything better?"

This was almost too much honesty.

"What do you want?" I asked hesitantly. "From me?"

"I want us to date," he said simply. "I want to go to bed with you sometimes. I want us to have a chance. If it doesn't work out, so be it. I can move back to California, I can get another teaching job, anything. I'm self-supporting, and I can work anywhere. So right now, I want to work here in Lawrenceton."

I couldn't seem to move. After a year of feeling empty, suddenly I felt full. After a year of grief, suddenly I felt a secret sort of joy. And I was terrified. I never could seem to do relationships like anyone else.

"Go look down the hall," I said. I pointed to the cabinet-lined hall leading out of the kitchen. He obediently strolled in that direction. I followed him. He looked at the cabinets approvingly, and then he opened the door at the end of the hall. The room had windows on three sides, and the morning light dazzled the eyes. The built-in bookcases that took up the remaining wall space were blindingly white with new paint. There were electric plugs in the floor where a desk would logically be placed, for a convenient computer plug-in.

A huge smile lit up Robin's face, and he spun to face me. "Come here," he said, falling to his knees and opening his arms. I crept over to him. He wrapped his arms around my waist, hugging me so tightly it almost hurt. I laughed and laughed. Then he kissed me, and I stopped laughing.

The phone rang about thirty minutes later. I had forgotten my cell phone was in my purse, and the little tune it played jogged me out of a lovely fog. Robin reached one long arm over to hook the shoulder strap of the purse. He dragged it over. I rummaged in it and fished out the phone.

"Yes?" I said.

"Roe, this is Sam," my boss said.

I tried to focus. I put my glasses on; everyone knows you can hear better over the phone if you're wearing your specs. "What can I do for you, Sam?" I asked.

"You sound funny," he said. "Were you asleep?"

"Oh, no," I said, my voice relaxed and slow. "No. Not asleep."

"I need you to do me a favor," Sam said.

"What's the matter?" I asked, finally picking up on the worry in his voice.

"It's Patricia. She didn't come in to work this morning, and she doesn't answer my calls."

"Gosh, that's not like her."

"No, it's not. She hasn't missed a day of work since I hired her. Her son's not in school, either. The school called here, looking for her."

"So what do you want me to do?"

"I want you to go over to her house and make sure everything's all right there."

"So, if there's a dead body, you don't care if I find it!"

"Roe," he protested, obviously offended. "I can't leave. It's work hours."

I sighed, not making any attempt to cover up my exasperation. Robin bent over me, doing something that made me bite my lip to keep in a gasp. "In a few minutes," I said, to get Sam off the phone. "I'll go, Sam, in a few minutes."

"Good," he said, obviously surprised I'd caved so quickly. He gave me the address. "Then let me know."

I hung up without saying good-bye. Sam wouldn't even notice.

Robin went with me, once I'd explained the circumstances to him.

I'd never known where Patricia lived before today. Of course I'd known where the street was. It was on the upper end of the scale for the largely black area of Lawrenceton that ran on the northwest side of town, literally following the old railroad tracks. Patricia's rental was a small, square house with minimal yard and no carport. Patricia's little car was nowhere in sight. There were two newspapers lying by the front steps.

I knocked, of course, but I didn't expect an answer, and I got none. I tried to peer in the windows but, literally, I wasn't up to that. Robin obligingly undertook the task, and he reported that the house looked very clean, but a little disordered—as though the Bledsoes had packed very quickly. The kitchen counter held none of the usual small appliances. A set of keys lay on the counter, along with a sheaf of money.

"Like she left the keys and the next month's rent so the landlord wouldn't feel any need to track her down," Robin said.

"Oh, *man,*" I muttered, trying not to moan. "This isn't going to be pretty," I told Robin as I punched in the library number.

Of course, Sam was distraught when I told him Patricia was gone. He could not believe she would just cut and run with no warning.

"Did you do something to her?" he said accusingly.

I'd had enough. "Sam," I said sharply into the phone, "Patricia may have been the perfect secretary, but I am the one who's worked for you for ten years. I think you should have a little faith in me." We hung up on each other, equally unhappy. I was cudgeling my brain to think of what could have happened to Patricia and Jerome. It was eerie and frightening to admit that she had evidently packed up her clothes and some small goods, and vanished.

"Come to think of it," I said to Robin, "she's been acting funny for days. Ever since she found out that the movie people attracted the media, and Celia came into the library and actually checked out books, Patricia's been asking questions like crazy about where the filming was going to be every day, whether the movie people would be coming to the library, like that."

"Do you think she's running from something? Maybe she knows someone on the crew," Robin said. "Someone she didn't want to recognize her?"

I considered. "Maybe," I said. "Or maybe she was scared she'd be noticed by one of the media people here to watch the filming and do interviews."

"Did you say anything about the film yesterday?"

"Nope," I said. "But she practically fainted when she saw me repairing a book. As a matter of fact, it was right after that that she left the library in a mighty big hurry."

"What was the book?"

"It was one Celia had checked out. You know, when she came to the library after she first got to Lawrenceton. I think she was looking for me, to have a peek at me. But she thrilled Sam by taking out a library card and checking out some books to do research for her next movie."

"The sixties-radical movie," Robin said.

"Right. *Bell-bottoms and Bombs,* or something like that."

"Can you find the book again?"

"Sure. Let's go to the library."

I tracked down the book in record time. It had been reshelved. I flipped it open, Robin looking over my shoulder. I turned to the picture section and began to really examine the old pictures. Lots of Afros and jeans, dashikis and beads. Peace signs. And photographs of wires and bits of hardware that were used in the making of bombs. What an incongruous blend, the philosophy of world peace, disarmament, and the construction of bombs to blow a hole in the consciousness of middle America.

The next picture was of a group of radicals at some rally. *Right to left,* read the caption, *suspected bomb makers Joanne Cheney, Ralph "Coco" Defarge, his teenage sister Anita, Maxwell Brand, and Barbara "Africa" Palley.*

"Anything ring a bell?" Robin asked in my ear, making me twitch.

"No. Yes," I said suddenly. I put my index finger on the picture of the radicals. "Look at the little sister."

"I never met Patricia Bledsoe," Robin reminded me.

"This is her," I said breathlessly. "Oh my God. Patricia the perfect helped her big brother make bombs in the sixties." I had to put my hands over my mouth to stifle a totally inappropriate laugh. Patricia, the rigorously traditional woman whose middle name was conservative! Patricia, who wouldn't even let her son wear Nike! "This is just going to kill Sam Clerrick," I said, suppressing a snort with great difficulty.

"This is funny, how?" Robin asked.

I tried to explain.

"Are you going to tell someone?" he asked.

"I have to, don't I?" I asked. "Don't I have to tell someone? She obviously picked up and ran because she thought I'd smoked her out. It couldn't have been further from the truth. If she'd just stayed put, I'd never have known."

"All the way back in the sixties," Robin said gently.

"Yeah, I know," I said, reluctant to debate my duty. "I have a lot of sympathy for her, even if she was the biggest pain in the patootie I've ever encountered. Except maybe Sam himself. But you know—if she did help build that bomb—I'm not trying to be Rhonda Righteous, but a security guard got killed, Robin. Besides, obviously Patricia was panicked by the idea of Celia seeing this picture and noticing the likeness, just like we did. What if Patricia somehow made her way onto the set and killed Celia, thinking Celia had spotted her and was going to tell?"

"Can't take that lightly," he agreed. "Will you tell Sam?"

"Oh, you bet," I said instantly. Then I reconsidered. "At least about our suspecting she's Anita Defarge."

"Not about her connection with Celia?"

"I know the papers this morning said it would have been easy for someone to have sneaked up to her trailer and killed her because there were a lot of people around. I just don't see it happening," I said. "Do you agree? There were a lot of people, but none of them looked or dressed like Patricia. And Celia had never talked to her, that I know of. They'd just glimpsed each other when Sam gave Celia a tour of the library. Wouldn't Celia have raised a fuss if someone she didn't know entered her trailer? She wouldn't have just sat there and waited for something bad to happen."

"I agree, for the most part," Robin said. "Just mention the fact you're most sure of; that the picture looks like his secretary."

"That's what I'll do," I said resolutely. I folded immediately. "In fact, maybe I'll leave calling the police up to him."

Robin waited out in the employee break room while I went in to Sam's office and broke the news. The fluorescent lights glinted off Sam's thick glasses as he looked hopelessly down at the black-and-white picture. "She was so great," he all but whimpered. "She took all my calls. I never had to talk to anybody. She understood the paperwork. She was never late. She was never sick. Her son was respectful and quiet."

"I'm sorry, Sam," I said as gently as I could. "I'll just leave it up to you what to do."

"Oh, there's no doubt about what to do," he said gloomily. "She may have been on the run all these years, always looking over her shoulder. And with the boy, too—I wonder what she told him. But I have to call the FBI. That's the law, and I have to uphold the law."

I felt like a second-class moral citizen compared to Sam's straightforward conviction. It must be wonderful to always know what was right to do.

At the back of my mind, I kept hoping that Patricia would walk in with some explanation of where she'd been and what she'd been doing. It wouldn't take much to satisfy Sam. If she just said, "What coincidence, that girl looks like a young me," that would probably do it. But the combined evidence of the flight and the picture—well, at least that should be investigated.

With a grim face, Sam picked up his phone to call the local police. He said, "I guess they can give me the right number to call." Then he put the phone back on its cradle. "But you know…maybe I don't have to call right now. After all, she still might show up. Maybe there's a sick relative she had to visit."

Maybe there was an elephant in my locker. I didn't know whether to laugh or cry. "Excuse me, Sam," I said. "I'll leave. You do what you think is right."

"Aren't you supposed to come in for the afternoon?"

"Yes."

"Then I'll see you later."

No "thank you," no "I appreciate it." Well, that was Sam. No people skills.

Robin was still waiting for me. He opened his mouth to ask a question, but I lifted a finger to my lips. When we were safely out in the parking lot, I told him what had transpired. He shook his head doubtfully, but agreed that Sam should be the one to make the phone call that would set law enforcement on Patricia's—Anita's—trail.

I had two hours before I was due back at the library, and we trailed over to Mother's office to sign some paperwork.

Mother greeted Robin quite matter-of-factly, but she was not overwhelmingly friendly, even when he asked her to find him a modest rental. She looked relieved, but not enthralled. She'd have to have warm-up time, I guessed. I wasn't going to push it.

My mother saw Robin as a potential threat to my peace of mind, a possible dumper of her vulnerable daughter, the potential dumpee. His fame and fortune made no difference at all to her. But a couple of the other realtors were more impressed. I thought Patty Cloud, now a partner and divorced twice, was going to come clean across her desk and tackle Robin, she was so enraptured with having a real celebrity in the office. She made a determined attempt to impress him with her attractiveness and her business acumen, and I was pleased to see that she didn't make a dent. Patty had always played one-up with me—a one-sided game, since I had never had a competitive bone in my body. I hoped Patty had gotten something out of it, because it had never made a bit of difference to me.

"I'll be glad to take you around town, get you set up with the bank and a dry cleaner and so forth," she offered, her eyes gleaming. Robin reached over to take my hand, very casually. "Roe is taking care of me," he said. Patty's face was just wonderful. She could think of about twelve bitchy things to say, but she couldn't, because, after all, I was the boss's daughter.

"Thanks," I said, when we were returning to my car.

He knew full well what I meant, but he just smiled his crooked smile. "It was my pleasure," he said, wiggling his eyebrows, and I laughed out loud.

He went back to his motel room to work, and I went home to make phone calls. Mother had worked it so I could move out of this house and into the house on McBride in a week. I called a company on the outskirts of Atlanta, made a definite date for them to come pack up this house on one day, and move the contents to the new place the next. It only cost me an arm and a leg and one kidney. I tried to ignore the stab of pain I felt as I thought of leaving this house empty. I tried instead to focus on the incoming family, with their son who would love living out in the country. He might make friends with my neighbor's dog Robert. Maybe Robert would stop his nighttime howling when the new family moved in. Speaking of Robert, he was doing some daytime howling now.

As I was pulling on some nicer pants to wear to work, I thought I heard a noise downstairs. I stopped breathing to listen better, while my fingers automatically pushed the button through the hole. I took some silent steps to the top of the stairs and listened. There it was again, a step in the hall.

I knew it was not Robin or my mother or anyone who had a reason to be there. I thought of Tracy, her angry face, and I stepped back into the bedroom and lifted the phone. I heard a familiar *beep beep beep*— somewhere downstairs, a receiver was off the hook. I needed my cell phone.

It was in my purse, which was on the counter in the kitchen downstairs.

"Aurora!" called a familiar voice from downstairs.

My breath gushed out in a sigh of sheer relief. Catherine Quick. It was her afternoon. Oh, thank God.

"Catherine," I called, trotting down the stairs, half angry and half delighted, "why did you come in so quiet? You could tell I was home."

I came into the kitchen to get yet another shock. Tracy, Robin's biggest fan, was holding a knife to Catherine's neck.

"Oh," I said quietly. "Oh."

Catherine's face was contorted with fear, and tears were running down her cheeks. I didn't blame her. The knife Tracy was gripping was a Swiss Army type thing, as far as I could tell—not a butcher knife, or a Bowie knife. But the blade looked plenty long enough to penetrate a vital area. It would never make it through air-port security, for example, I told myself crazily. My thoughts were trying to escape from the here and now.

"You ruined it," Tracy said. "He was just on the verge, I could tell! He was just on the verge of asking me out."

"You're right," I said instantly. She had to be made to let go of Catherine. That Catherine should be in-volved in this at all was simply atrocious. Catherine was in her sixties, had high blood pressure, and should not be subjected to this deranged woman.

Of course, I shouldn't be, either.

My purse was on the counter, right by the side door, where I had a habit of dropping it. Tracy, her auburn hair falling in snakes around her head, was between my purse and me.

"Did you kill Celia?" I asked, before I thought. Obviously.

She laughed. "I hit her with the statue. She earned her own death."

"But she was already dead," I said, compounding my error.

"She was asleep," said Tracy, frowning. Her face was dirty. She was a far cry from the spic-and-span food provider in her spotless white, the woman I'd met such a few days ago. Could people really crumble that quickly?

"Right," I said hastily. Tracy wanted to take credit for Celia. And if I lived, I'd be glad to tell the police she'd done her best to kill Celia. It was just that some-one had beaten her to it.

"For months, I've been planning this," Tracy said.

"Planning…?"

"Meeting Robin Crusoe. Getting him to love me. Ever since I saw the picture on his Web site."

It was news to me that Robin had a Web site. "Which picture? The picture of Robin and Celia at the Emmys?"

"Yes, right when it first came out. Did you notice the way she was ignoring him? She didn't even care that she was out with a brilliant writer. She's a slut; there's a mil-lion actresses in the world who can do what she does. But Robin's a writer in a million. I've read every single book he's ever written. Ten times apiece, I bet!" Her face was soft and dreamy, but the knife looked just as sharp. "I've got every short story, in every language. I've got every interview, on-line and in print."

"You probably know more about Robin than I'll ever know." I was quite willing to concede that. I edged a little forward and to one side. The kitchen table was no longer between us, which I regretted, but I was a lit-tle closer to the cell phone.

"You're damn straight I do. So what are you doing going to bed with him?"

It was dumb to be embarrassed in front of Cath-erine, but I was. As if she cared, at this point. "How do you know what I'm doing?" I asked instead.

"I was in the backyard of your new house this morning," she said, so choked with fury I was terrified all over again.

It made me sick to think of her watching Robin and me. I also felt a little surprised she hadn't broken in on us then.

"He wouldn't like me if he saw me kill you," she said, as if she'd heard my thoughts.

"No, he wouldn't." Let's make that perfectly clear.

"But then, if no one finds out, I would get to comfort him when you die."

Okay, so this wasn't getting any better. "Don't you think Robin would know?" I asked.

"He doesn't know about Celia." She looked smug.

"He went to the police, to tell them he suspected you."

I didn't know if saying that was smart or not, but to tell the truth, I needed to find something that worked, and in a hurry.

"Did he really? But I did it for him." She looked more than a little confused. "I'm glad I didn't go back home last night. I got a room in the motel where he's staying. I couldn't get a room on the same floor, because all the movie people are taking up that floor, but I got a room right below him." She sighed. "I lay awake all night, thinking about him."

Hoo, boy. This gal would be spending some time in the loony bin, for sure. I had eased more than a foot closer during her meanderings.

"He's very attractive," I said sincerely, "but I'll bet you need some sleep."

"I can't sleep," she told me, sounding peeved about it. "I just keep waking up. And I know he's there, just out of reach. I need him. I deserve him." She gestured with the knife, and Catherine made a strangled sound.

"And I'm gonna have him," Tracy said quietly.

Quick as a wink, she shoved Catherine to one side and lunged for me with the knife.

Even in those few short minutes, I'd accepted a status quo, and the sudden change in threat caught me off guard. Catherine went reeling across the kitchen, and I yelled, "The phone! It's in my purse!" before Tracy grabbed me by the hair and began trying to stab me. I screamed and ducked, and she missed me with her first attempt. My scalp stung with the pull on my hair. She swung again, and this time she cut me below my shoulder. My knees folded from the shock of it.

The blood was immediate and it distracted her long enough for me to yank away from her—leaving her in possession of a handful of my hair—and drop to the floor. I rolled under the kitchen table, knocking the chairs out of the way. She staggered a little as a chair rocked against her and then fell to the floor with a huge clatter. She was still trying to get her balance. Without any planning on my part, my hands shot out from under the table to grab Tracy's ankles, and I yanked with all my strength. Down she crashed, with a shriek of her own, and then she gave a low moan and lay still.

After a long, shocked second of watching Tracy's blood flow onto my kitchen floor, I realized she'd fallen on her knife. I backed out from under the table so I'd be on the other side. I pelted out of that kitchen so fast I don't think my feet hit the steps down to the walkway. Catherine was outside, already talking to the dispatcher, though she was almost incoherent with shock.

"Where is she?" Catherine screamed.

"She's hurt, she's on the floor!"

"Oh my Lord! Did you hear that?" she demanded, and I heard the raised voice on the other end of the line.

"I have to go now, she might get up," Catherine said. She turned off the phone. But she managed to tell me the cops were on the way, and she helped me scramble into her car. We locked the doors while we waited.

We had about three minutes before the police could get there, and at first we didn't say a word to each other, being occupied with important things like breathing and praying. Oh, and I was bleeding. Catherine grabbed a kitchen towel from a basket of wash in the backseat and folded it into a pad, and I pressed it to my wound. Finally, when our gasps were down to pants, Catherine said, "I didn't have any choice but to bring her in, Aurora. She held that knife on me, and I just thought about my kids and grandkids, and I let her in with my key."

"I don't blame you one bit," I said sincerely. "I would have done the same thing."

"I tried to make a little noise," Catherine said. "To warn you. As much as I could."

"Thank you. At least I suspected something was wrong when I came down the stairs."

"Praise God we lived through that," Catherine said, sounding surprised by the fact.

"I don't know if she did," I said in a small voice. "I think she hurt herself pretty bad, falling on that knife."

"I know I will have to pray God for forgiveness, but right now, I just don't give a damn."

"Actually, I vote along with you," I said.

"Can't you stay out of trouble?" bellowed the new sheriff as he drew his gun and eased up to the side of the house. I rolled down the window to point at the open kitchen door, as if Sheriff Coffey couldn't see it himself.

Padgett Lanier had had a massive heart attack in his office (some said while he was receiving the personal attentions of an attractive prisoner) the previous spring, and his newly elected successor was a politically savvy African-American named Davis Coffey. Coffey, who was six feet tall and massive, had been out here a couple of times before during his years as deputy.

Jimmy Henske and Levon Suit, who had also paid visits to my house before, gave me disapproving headshakes as they followed their leader. Levon winked at me, though.

After calling into the house and getting no response, David Coffey hurled his large body into the doorway we'd left open, gun at the ready. After a few minutes, I could see through the kitchen window that he'd lowered his gun and was looking down at the floor.

The ambulance came up the drive just as Catherine

and I scrambled out of her car, an aged Buick. It was for Tracy, Davis not having noticed I was wounded. Levon and Jimmy had stepped out of the house to wait in the yard, and Levon winced when he saw the blood dripping down my left arm. Jimmy raised his radio to his mouth and, in only a few minutes, another ambulance arrived for me. I knew my wound wasn't anywhere near life-threatening—it was probably pretty minor—but it hurt like hell, and I couldn't seem to stop the bleeding.

Tracy was alive, I could tell. Her mouth was moving when they were loading her into the ambulance, and though I couldn't hear what she was saying, I was sure it was about Robin.

Who, by the way, I should call. He picked up the phone at the motel and said, "Yes?" abstractedly. It was his working voice. Well, he'd just have to put it aside for now.

I explained the situation to him briefly. There was a moment of silence, a silence I couldn't characterize. Then he said, "I'll meet you at the hospital," and the phone went dead.

By the time we got there, I was feeling a little spacey. Loss of blood and shock, I guess. Plus, the EMT who rode in back with me took my glasses off, for some reason, and I am never at my most alert when the whole world is a blur. He was a handsome young man, whose family had emigrated from El Salvador, he told me. He had a crewcut and a large tattoo, but I was willing to love him nonetheless. I had to admit our romance was doomed when he passed the time on our ride to the hospital by telling me about his motorcycle.

I would have been glad to ride into town in Catherine's car instead of the ambulance, but (a) I didn't want to get blood all over it, and (b) she didn't offer. It was possible Catherine had had enough of me for one day and, frankly, I couldn't blame her.

Robin was already at the emergency room entrance, and he behaved in a gratifyingly loverlike way. Not a disappointment, like my EMT. Robin was even a practical help, which I hadn't expected. He fished my insurance cards out of my purse and showed them to the admitting clerk.

"Thank you," I said, wondering if my voice was as fuzzy as my vision. "This is above and beyond the…" And then I didn't know how to finish the sentence.

"Obligation of a new boyfriend?" Robin suggested.

"Something like that," I agreed, trying to smile. "I started to throw you over for the cute Hispanic guy who rode with me in the ambulance, but I think you'll do."

"Glad to hear it."

The emergency room doctor was a gruff young woman employed by one of the big health-care systems. She had one of the worst haircuts I'd ever seen, but she had a massive assurance that I really liked. She let you know that she was not about to make a mistake, and you would get worse at your peril.

"Don't see too many knife wounds in Lawrenceton,"

she commented. I had my head turned away, since I just didn't want to look.

"Mmmm," she said after a painful few moments. "Well, I'm gonna numb you up; you need some stitches."

Robin winced. "You can leave," I told him, wishing I could, too. "There's no need for you to watch this."

"Are you the husband?" the doctor asked.

I opened my mouth to say my husband was dead, and then I shut it.

"I'm the boyfriend," Robin said. His charm was such that she grinned at him before she strode out of the room.

"That what you are?" I asked weakly.

"I don't know what to call what I am, so that'll do."

A nurse came in and gave me a shot, with the customary warning about me feeling a little pinch. I rolled my eyes at Robin. Whatever getting a shot felt like, a little pinch was not it.

"This really hurts," I told Robin, "and I'm really ready for the shot to work."

"Do you need to think about something else?" he asked.

"That would help. I wonder how Tracy is. She tried to kill me!" I said, amazed all over again. "Did I tell you she was watching this morning?"

Robin turned red. "While we…?"

"Yes, while we."

"Oh, God." His face scrunched with revulsion.

"Yeah, me too."

"But it was great, wasn't it?" he said, bending closer. "You want to think about that while the doctor takes these stitches?"

"It would be better than thinking about someone actually sewing on me."

"Do you remember how you…" he whispered in my ear, and then the doctor came in. She began her work, chatting all the time to Robin, but I kept my eyes fixed on his face, and I knew he was thinking about that morning, too.

When she was through she gave me a list of instructions and told me I could go. Robin rescued my glasses and we left the hospital. I glanced at Robin doubtfully from time to time. This was surely a lot of trouble for a fragile new relationship.

Robin opened his car door for me, and went around to the driver's side. After he got in, he put the key in the ignition, but then he paused. "I know you're tired right now, but I need to talk to you."

Oh, no. Here it came. "Sure," I said, my voice empty of emotion.

"I feel guilty as hell. Tracy said she hit Celia with the Emmy?"

"Yeah."

"And she attacked you. It seems like I bring nothing but trouble to a relationship."

"I was just thinking the same thing about myself."

His eyebrows raised in a question.

"My first long-term boyfriend marries someone else

and then divorces, my first husband dies, my short-term boyfriend shows back up and there's a killer stalking him."

He laughed. When Robin laughed, his whole thin face was involved. "I left my short-term girlfriend behind, hooked up with my agent, had a disastrous relationship with her, dated an actress who was strictly out for herself, then went back to my short-term girlfriend to get her stabbed, apparently."

"Can we actually date without killing each other?"

"I think we have to try," he said.

"I think I need to go to sleep," I said.

Robin took me back home, and helped me undress and get into bed. Okay, maybe that was overdoing it a little, but I think a woman deserves some bed rest after she's been stabbed. I called the library to tell Sam I wouldn't be coming in on time. I explained why in as few words as I could manage. He was so miserable he hardly seemed to care.

Robin said he'd be downstairs with his laptop, and I snuggled down in the bed. I could hardly believe it was only early afternoon. The morning had been packed with more incidents that I usually encountered in a week. Maybe two weeks. I'd had great sex, found out a coworker was a terrorist, started buying a house, and been stabbed in my kitchen. Busy day.

And it wasn't over yet.

I woke up about four. My arm was very sore, but it was bearable as long as I didn't move it too vigorously. I got

some pants on by myself, and actually zipped and buttoned them. Getting the nightgown off over my head
was much worse, and pulling on a knit shirt was just as
bad. But finally I managed, and crept downstairs very
slowly.

Robin was asleep on my couch, his laptop plugged
in on my desk. He'd carried my phone to the couch
with him, and it was moving up and down with the
gentle rise and fall of his chest. He snored, like a big
cat. It was a large noise, but oddly delicate.

I padded into the kitchen barefoot, and made some
coffee. I looked outside to see a day that had gone
gray and windy. Rain was coming up. I watched a
swirl of gum leaves sweep past the window, yellow
and red and brown. Indian summer was definitely
over. I looked at the thermometer mounted outside
the window. It had dropped twenty degrees since this
morning.

While the coffee perked, I found a notepad with
messages in Robin's slanted, narrow handwriting. My
mother had called, which was no surprise. I should
have called her. My sister-in-law—well, my stepsister-
in-law—had called, too. So had Sally. And Arthur.

The last name Robin had written was "Will Weir."
I wondered what the cameraman could have to say to
me. Though everyone else deserved to be called back
before Will, his was the number I dialed first, out of
sheer curiosity.

"Weir," he answered. I knew he must be on a cell

phone, but it was the best connection I'd ever had. No crackling, no distant buzz.

"You called me?" I asked, after I identified myself.

"Right. The newspaper reporter who was here today, doing a story for your local paper…she said that a woman who claims to have killed Celia had attacked you. Is that true?"

"Yes," I said, promising myself I'd grab Sally Allison and stuff her head in a food processor. Violent images were coming easily to me today. "It was Tracy, the young woman who served the food at the caterer's truck?"

"The reddish-haired girl," he said, after waiting a second for his memory to kick in, I assumed.

"That's her."

"Why did she say that?"

I looked at the phone. I was glad Will couldn't see that look. "Well, because she had a bee in her bonnet about Robin Crusoe, and she was resentful of Celia's former relationship with him."

"But why would she attack you?"

This had me stumped. "She thinks that Robin and I have a relationship now," I said, feeling very awkward.

"That is a little quick," he said, his voice as dry as toast.

"Robin and I are old friends," I said, as neutrally as possible.

"I remember, from the book. Well, Mark and Joel wanted to know if it was because of something that happened on the set…"

"No," I said, not following his line of reasoning, but willing to dismiss it as my own woolly-headedness.

"Mark brought some books by the library yesterday," Will was saying.

"Yes."

"Some books Celia had borrowed?"

"Yes."

"They were in her trailer when she was killed?"

Were we playing twenty questions here? Robin slouched into the kitchen, his hair rumpled and his face creased from the throw pillow on the couch. He came up behind me and wrapped his long arms around me. I snuggled back against him.

"Yes," I said again, hoping he'd get to the point soon. I tapped his name on the list with my finger, so Robin would know to whom I was speaking. I could feel him nod.

"The thing is, she'd borrowed some books from me," Will was saying.

"Oh, gosh. No wonder you want to know about the books." I never loaned books, myself. You never got them back, or if you did they had peanut-butter fingerprints on them, or smelled of other people's cigarettes or pets. "Aside from a batch of paperbacks, there were two hardbacks about the sixties, and one home health book. Those were Lawrenceton library books, though. I'm really sure."

"A home health book?" His voice sounded weaker.

"Yeah, the kind that you use when you want to diagnose your own illness. Poor thing."

"You think she figured out what she had?" Weir sounded horrified.

"I know she had. There was a bookmark on the page for Huntington's chorea."

A long silence fell. Robin poured himself a mug of coffee, asked me in mime if I wanted one, too. I nodded emphatically.

"She knew," Will repeated, his voice just as shocked as it had been the first time. "Oh, my God."

"I'm sorry if I've upset you," I said, actually feeling a little on the impatient side. "What books were you trying to find?" I took a sip of coffee. The groggy nap hangover began to fade. My eyes strayed to my other phone messages. I had a lot of things to do, and my arm was burning.

"Books," he said blankly. "Oh, right, I'd loaned her some paperbacks. You said Mark also brought a few paperbacks to the library."

"Yes, that's what I said." He could have asked Mark before he called me.

"I'll drop by the library and have a look through those books," he said. "They're not important, but I stuck a letter in one of them, and I need it. When will you be working?"

"Tonight, six to nine," I said. I'd told Sam I'd try to at least make the evening part of my shift, if I could. I didn't feel too bad.

"If we finish filming, I'll drop by," he said.

"Okay," I said doubtfully. "They're in a box in the

back. By the employee entrance, but it'll be locked, so come to the main doors. I can show you." I was sure no one had had a chance to get to them in the past twenty-four hours.

"Good, maybe I'll get there tonight." He sounded much more relaxed than he had at the beginning of the conversation.

"You're going in to work tonight?" Robin asked after I'd hung up.

"I ought to," I said. "I really don't hurt too bad, and with Patricia missing, I feel like I should keep things as even as possible. I'll call Sam to tell him as soon as I finish my coffee."

"I was hoping you'd stay with me," Robin said, doing his best to look pitiful.

"We've had our time today," I reminded him. "I think after work I'll need to come home and sleep some more. My arm is sore." Plus other things.

He kissed my shoulder. "Did that make it feel better?"

I tried not to smile, failed. "A little."

"Can we plan on tomorrow night?"

"Oh, yes. And I don't have to work the next day."

He smiled at me. Robin had a radiant smile.

We talked about the move for a while, and the book Robin was working on, while I returned the rest of my phone calls.

Sam was glad to hear I was coming in, since he hadn't found anyone to replace me yet. After an incident a few years ago, librarians weren't allowed to work by themselves, no matter how few patrons showed up in the evening. My mother was glad to hear I was all right, and she had some rental units to show Robin. My stepsister-in-law Poppy was glad, too, and she wanted me to know that Brandon had his very first tooth. Arthur wanted me to know that law-enforcement gossip had it that Tracy was talking at great length about everything: her long-standing obsession with Robin, beginning with reading his books and escalating to focus on his personal life, her careful maneuvering to get the job with Molly's Moveable Feasts, her visit to Celia's trailer with a tray of croissants as camouflage, her subsequent movements...

"That's good," I said, puzzled.

"She's telling us everything," he repeated, significantly. "In detail."

I could feel my face turn red as I realized Arthur was telling me that everyone in the SPACOLEC (Spalding County Law Enforcement Complex) was aware that Robin and I had had sex on the carpet in the office of the house I was buying.

"Oh," I said. My voice sounded small and embarrassed to my own ears.

"Oh," he said. Angry.

"Um. Well, I'll talk to you later, thanks for letting me know—I think."

"Roe, you realize this woman did not really kill Celia Shaw?"

"Yes, I know that." Point?

"You want to know what I think?"

"No."

"I think your new boyfriend did it. I think he knew what disease she had and killed her out of mercy."

"I think you're *nuts,*" I said furiously, and slammed the phone down.

But when Robin asked me what I'd gotten upset about, I didn't look him in the face. And I didn't explain. No one could have persuaded me to believe Robin murdered someone...anyone—out of malice. But out of pity...it was almost conceivable. A lovely young woman, once beloved, facing a horrible fate— it was just barely possible. Didn't the fact that she'd been drugged argue that whoever had killed her didn't want her to feel the pain? Didn't the pillow pressed over her face give her a comparatively gentle end? Celia Shaw had had a merciful murder, if you believed such a thing was possible.

I didn't know Robin well enough, really, to completely rule out such a possibility. I needed to be by myself: to think, to recover my equilibrium. I reminded myself vigorously that Robin had a practically ironclad alibi.

He left a few minutes later, and we planned on seeing each other the next day, and I smiled at him, but when I locked the door behind him, I have to confess I felt some relief. When I thought of him not only coming to the hospital, but taking such good care of me afterward, I knew I was being one horrible woman to even doubt him for a second. But the tiny thread of doubt made me miserable, and I didn't need to be around him for a while.

I could not have a relationship with someone who could do such a thing. On the other hand, when I thought of the dreadful disease that would have killed Celia slowly, maybe her death had been a favor to her. That didn't mean I could cohabit with the one who'd granted it.

I pottered around, cleaning our mugs and the coffee-pot, taking some extra-strength pain reliever the hospital had sent home with me, cleaning myself up a little for work. By five-thirty, I was at least presentable and functioning, though at a low level. Jeans and a long-sleeved tee were not my usual working gear, but I was not about to try to change again. I put on my red-framed glasses, to give me pep, and brushed my hair awkwardly. With the damp and cold in the air, my hair was on its worst behavior. It made a cloud around me, crackling with electricity.

It was already dark when I used my key to enter the employee door of the library, always kept locked after dark. The lights were on in the employee lounge, and I glanced over to see the books Mark Chesney had brought in, still in their box on the repair table. Patricia's office was still dark. I wondered how far away she'd gotten by now, and I felt sorry for Jerome. As I slung my purse into my locker, I thought of how long Patricia had kept such a big secret, and how careful she must have had to be for many years. A slip of the tongue, and her new life and her son would be gone.

Celia had had a massive secret, too. I wondered if she had known that her mother had died of the same disease she was developing. I wondered how she'd gone to work the first few days of filming, knowing what she was facing and how terrible her end would be: that surely her disease would become apparent to everyone in the course of time. I found myself thinking that Celia had surely had a theatrical flair, and she would have appreciated being a colorful True Crime episode rather than a disease of the week.

Lindsey Russell, a very young woman who'd just recently begun working as the children's librarian, passed through on her way out the back door. She gave me a cheerful wave, and told me the library had been really quiet all afternoon. Lindsey wasn't in the gossip loop yet, I gathered. I smiled back at her, and told her to have a good evening.

I strolled into the main part of the library, and discovered I was working with Perry. A few years before, it would have made me quite nervous to be alone with him. The money Sally had spent on him, or Perry's own determination to get well, or time itself, had gone far toward curing Perry of his many problems.

Perry was thin and nervous, but he was also a lot more sociable than he'd been, and he'd licked his drug problems. His relationships with women didn't seem to last too long, but wasn't that always the case until you found the One? I didn't always believe that there's a mate for every individual, but some days it was a real convenient and comforting concept.

"Hey, girl," Perry said. "I heard about your unexpected visitor. Was that the red-headed woman who was in here the other day, reading the magazines?"

"That was Tracy, all right. And she was the one who knocked me down in the parking lot, I'm sure."

"It was a woman, after all. You were right. How's the arm?"

"It's sore, but I'm going to be fine. No muscle damage to speak of."

"That's good. I can't believe you came in to work."

"I hated to stress Sam out any more than he's already stressed."

"So, you know Patricia left?"

I nodded cautiously. I didn't know what story Sam had told to give her a head start.

"Sam thinks she'll come back. If he wasn't already married, and if doing a mixed-race relationship wouldn't be so out of Sam's league, I'd say he was in love with that woman."

Immediately, I felt something click, and I knew Perry was right.

Ultraconventional, ultraconservative lily white Sam Clerrick, married and the father of two, was in love with African-American left-wing former-bombmaker Anita Defarge. If she was his soulmate, God truly had a sense of humor.

I shook my head to clear it. "Perry," I said, "do we actually have any work to do?"

"I guess you could be entering the patron requests,"

he said, with a sigh. That was a nothing job, recording the patron requests for specific books so we could fit them into our budget. "There's only one patron in the building, Josh Finstermeyer. He's over in periodicals."

I grinned at Josh's name, and Perry looked at me oddly. "Oh, by the way, Roe," he said, and he sounded so elaborately casual that I went on the alert immediately. "You know the man who brought those books in yesterday?"

"Mark Chesney?"

"One of the movie people."

"Yes, the assistant director."

"Do you know him very well?"

"Hardly at all. He seems nice enough. I don't think working for Joel Park Brooks would be a job for the faint-hearted."

Perry was fiddling with some reserved books. I waited to see what he'd say, with some curiosity.

"He came back in this morning," Perry said.

I tried to think of a neutral response. "Oh?" was all I could come up with. I had a feeling I was about to be confided in. Perry fiddled with the books some more. "Had he found some books he'd overlooked?" I prompted him.

"More things she'd checked out? No," Perry said. "He, ah, wanted to know if I'd go have a drink with him after work tonight."

"Okay." I shrugged. "Are you going?"

"I'd love to talk to him," Perry confessed. "Someone

who lives and works in Hollywood. God, that would be so interesting. You know, I've always loved to be in the community theater plays, and I've done a couple of things in Atlanta."

Actually, I had forgotten all about Perry's obsession with the theater.

"I'd always hoped I'd get a chance to talk to your stepson," Perry went on, "but he was only in town so briefly when he came, and I could tell you two didn't have a good relationship."

"That's putting it mildly."

"So now this Mark, wanting to talk to me, it just seems so…exciting."

"So go."

"But at the same time, it seems like a…date." Perry flushed dark red. "I mean, why me? Would a regular guy just make a point of coming in and inviting another guy out for a drink?"

In my opinion, no. But I felt totally unqualified to give Perry advice on this issue. I had long suspected Perry had so much trouble maintaining relationships with women because he was backing the wrong horse, orientation-wise—but I sure wasn't going to suggest that to him.

"If you want to go, go. It doesn't commit you to any-thing," I said at last. "If you don't have a good time, if something happens that—doesn't interest you, that you don't feel comfortable with, get up and leave." I shrugged again.

He brightened as if I'd given the date my blessing. "That's the right way to look at it," he said. "You're so wise, Roe."

That was me—the wise librarian of Lawrenceton, Georgia.

Our evening dragged. We were supposed to get off at nine, and at eight-thirty Perry excused himself to go through his getting-ready ritual, whatever that consisted of. I heard the drone of an electric razor from the men's restroom.

No one had shown a face in the library for the past hour, when Josh had left. I'd heard some books thud down into the book drop, but that was the most action we'd had. I began straightening the desk for the morning people. My arm was hurting, and I was looking forward to another pain pill and my own bed. The energy I'd recouped from the nap had long been used up, and I was very tired. I wondered where Robin was, what he was doing, whether he knew suspicion had crossed my mind. I wondered how Barrett was feeling, if he'd gotten over the shock of finding Celia dead. I wondered if he was a serious suspect in Celia's death.

While I was pondering all these things, I found a book with a number of loose pages. One of the day workers had put it on the cart to return to the stacks. I snorted with indignation. That book had to go back to the repair area.

"Mark's here!" Perry called. I turned to look at the front doors. Perry was wearing a black leather jacket and he looked really good. Mark was wearing a fresh shirt and creased khakis. "I'm going to go on and leave if that's okay with you, Roe."

It lacked only ten minutes till closing time. "Sure. All I have to do is lock the back door on my way out." I'd closed the library many times.

Perry and Mark waved as I locked the double glass doors behind them, and they strode off into the night. I began turning out lights in the main room. Of course, we kept some on all night, but that still left plenty to do. I looked around the big room, took one big inhalation of eau de book, and opened the heavy door that led to the new wing of the library. The employee lounge still smelled of Perry's cologne, and I decided that if Perry was putting on cologne and shaving for a drink with a guy, he wasn't as totally clueless of his own nature as he'd tried to appear. I got my purse out of my locker, extracted my keys, and spotted a light still burning in Sam's office. I went to switch it off. Now the employee lounge was the only lit room.

The building suddenly felt very empty, uncomfortably empty.

I heard someone fumbling at the lock outside and I stood in the middle of the floor, paralyzed with sudden fear. The door flew open, picked up by the wind outside. I realized as a leaf gusted in that it was beginning to rain again outside.

Patricia Bledsoe—I could not think of her by her real

name—stepped in from the dark. She was as astonished to see me as I was to see her.

"He hasn't called the police," I said instantly.

She gave a sigh. I thought it was of relief. "I saw your car in the parking lot, but I noticed two people came out the front. I thought you'd gone somewhere with Perry," she said. "Jerome's out in the car. We had to turn back halfway to…well, halfway, and come back. I forgot something important."

"Get whatever it is, don't mind me," I said. "I'm not even here." I'd dropped my purse on a table, and now I picked it up again. Patricia sped into her office, pulling a drawer out all the way and fumbling under it. Her hand came up clutching an envelope, and I realized she'd had it taped to the bottom of her drawer. How the paranoid live. Though, in Patricia's case, the paranoia was justified.

"Where will you go?" I asked. "Wait a minute, forget I asked that."

And we both heard the back door begin to open. Patricia hadn't locked it behind her.

With a desperate expression on her face, Patricia ducked down below her desk. I stepped out of her office, hoping the light in there didn't show anything suspicious over the half-wall.

To my surprise, Will Weir stepped in. I'd half-forgotten out conversation. His timing was awful.

"What are you doing here?" I asked, not caring if I sounded rude or not.

"I'm glad I caught you," he said, smiling. "I'm sorry if I scared you. Is it illegal, coming in the back way? The front was locked, and it's not nine yet."

No, it was all of 8:58. I felt abruptly uneasy. "You're not supposed to come in this door," I said. I didn't smile back. "You're going to have to wait to come to the library tomorrow. I've shut everything down."

"I just needed to see the books Mark brought in," he said, still smiling. "I see they're over here in the box."

"It's too late. You have to come back tomorrow."

"I have to work tomorrow. Let me just take a minute, and I'll be all through." He'd made his voice soothing, as though I was being childish.

I know when someone's trying to get away with something. I've sure been a librarian long enough for that.

"Will, what's in those books that's so important? That can't wait?"

He smiled again, made a "wait" gesture with his hand, and began riffling through the pile of books. The wind was whooshing through the cracked door, and it fluttered the pages of the book he held, the book about diagnosing your own illness. Will shook it. Nothing happened. He followed that procedure with every book in the box. As book after book proved a disappointment, he tossed them to one side. I almost protested, and then caught myself.

He kept talking the whole time, meaningless phrases like, "I'll be out of your hair in just a second," and "I just need to check these books." He was just trying to keep me sedated, I realized, and then he lifted the bound movie script that Mark had brought by accident. I'd completely forgotten it. Will turned it upside down, and shook it, and from its pages flew a folded piece of paper. The wind picked up the paper and blew it in my direction, and it landed on the table to my right.

Without a single thought in my head I picked it up and unfolded it. It was a yellowed letter, and it began, "Dearest Celia, the lawyer should give you this when you turn twenty-nine. I think you should know who your father is…" and then the paper was snatched out of my hand.

"You don't need that. It's mine." Will was smiling again, that warm and homey smile that had made me feel relaxed and comfortable in his company.

"Were you Celia's dad?" I asked, incredulous. "Did she know?"

"She did after the lawyer delivered that letter," Will said. "She turned twenty-nine last week, and the package came Federal Express from the lawyer in Wilmington."

"Why did Celia's mom leave her a letter?"

"She knew she wasn't going to be around to talk to Celia in person."

"She knew she had Huntington's."

"Yeah, she knew. 'Course, I didn't, until it was too late. I would never have risked a relationship with a woman who had a disease like that. I would have known my heart would get broken."

"So you knew Linda Shaw after her divorce?"

"Yeah, she came out to California to find me. She'd felt the first symptoms, and the Huntington's had been diagnosed in North Carolina. She wanted to see Celia placed before she got any worse, and she wanted to do a little living before she got too sick. So she left Celia with her sister, and she followed me out to California. She wanted to do that living with me. The only thing is, she didn't tell me. She didn't tell me she'd had my child, and she didn't tell me she was going to die." He was bitter all over: voice, stance, words.

"That was really wrong of her," I said softly. I began to edge a little closer to the door. He was still to my left, by the book-mending area, but with one leap he could be between me and freedom.

"Damn right." He looked as though he was going to cry. "Then, when she got really sick, she begged me to help her. She begged me to kill her. Finally, I helped her out."

"She wasn't a suicide."

"Not strictly speaking."

"It was you."

"Yes, it was me. She asked me. I couldn't stand to see her suffer any longer, lose her personality, her muscle control, everything that made Linda a person."

"What about Celia?"

He was scanning the letter. "I met up with her when she came out to California after she got a bit part in a TV series I was filming. She looked so much like her mother that I followed her the first time I saw her. Then I arranged to meet her. She was Linda's daughter, all right, and she was my daughter, too. At first she tried to make friends with me—she didn't know, of course. She just knew I was an important guy."

Oh. *That* was the kind of "friends" she'd tried to make.

"Luckily, I'd told her I was her dad before the letter came."

"You know, I really don't need to know any more," I said cheerfully. "You can take your letter and go now."

"I think you know a little more than you need to," he said. "I've taken care of the women I loved. I've done the right thing by them. I don't love you, and I don't care any more if I do the right thing or not. I like my job, and I like to work, and I don't want you to stop me doing that. Celia never told anyone we were kin."

"Who your family is, is your business."

"I don't think for one second that you're that naïve, Aurora. I think you know I killed Celia."

"Why?" I asked desperately. "Why would you do that?"

"You could tell she was getting it," he said. "You could tell. It was just like Linda. She was beginning to stumble around. She was beginning to make these sudden movements without knowing she was doing it. She was having trouble remembering her lines. In a year, she'd be just another starlet who'd caught a bad disease, and she'd be forgotten in two years. This way, she'll always be remembered. She'll always be brought up in the magazines. Like Brandon Lee. Freak accident; they still print his name, his picture, what might have been. Celia, they'll do the same."

The thing I hated most—media attention—he'd sought out as being preeminently desirable. More valuable than life. And yet, hadn't I had the same thought hours before? Better a provocative whodunit than a disease of the week?

"What would Celia have thought about that?"

"You can't tell me she didn't know," he said defensively. "I brought her the coffee with the Valium in it, a whopping dose; she must have tasted something funny about it. She just looked at me while she was drinking it. Then she closed her eyes and waited."

Then she fell unconscious.

"She'd had a good night before with that stepson of yours," Will Weir said. "He was good-looking enough, and self-serving enough, to show her a good time."

I wanted to throw up. The Celia Shaw pre-death lay.

"And she was on the set of her very own movie, her very first starring role. Her Emmy was beside her. She had her own trailer."

"So you put a pillow over her face."

"She didn't struggle. She was at peace. No disease, at the top of her form. And then I carried off the coffee cup."

I put a hand over my mouth. He explained what he'd done so plausibly, but it was wrong, wrong, wrong.

"Did you ask Celia what she wanted? Did you tell her about her mom's Huntington's?"

"Not before she read it in the letter." He shrugged. "I didn't know about the letter."

"Would you have told her?"

"No." He looked surprised. "No, I would never have told her. We'd have had to go through the whole emotional scene, then, the crying and shit."

The crying and shit. What an inconvenience.

"Did you get this job with the idea of watching over her?"

He said, "More or less."

Meaning, no. He'd been hired by chance, observed the beginnings of Celia's disease by chance, revealed his identity to her only when she'd made a play for him. And then, he thought he'd kill her. After all, he was her dad. He had the right to choose for her.

I don't think I've ever loathed anyone so much in my life.

"What are you going to do now?" I asked, cutting to the chase. I might as well know.

"I guess I'm going to take this letter with me. I guess, if you say anything about it, I'll just say you lied."

Hope flickered in me for a minute, to be extinguished when I considered the overwhelming selfishness of this man's life. He had no intention of leaving me alive with his secret. After all, there were blood tests that could prove whether or not he'd been Celia's father. And there was the lawyer who could testify he'd had a letter sent to Celia on her birthday, even if he couldn't say what the contents of that letter had been.

I had no idea what I could do to stop him. I don't go around armed. You'd be surprised how many Southern belles have a gun in their purse, but I wasn't one of them. I didn't have a stun gun, or a blackjack...hey. I had a panic button! It was on the keyless entry pad for my car. I'd gotten my keys out and now they were clutched in my hand. Was my car close enough to the back door to pick up the signal? I hadn't the slightest idea how the damn thing worked. I probably had to be closer. So, before I could have second thoughts, I made a dash for the back door, managed to get my hand out of it, and pressed the panic button.

Beep! Beep! Beep! My car responded in a wonderful way, lights flashing and horn blaring. But I feared it was too little, too late, because now Will had hold of me around the waist and was pulling me back into the library. I held on to the doorknob of the open door as long as I could, but he was a strong man and my grip was weak.

Who would be driving past the library anyway, at nine o'clock on a weeknight? Downtown Lawrenceton was pretty much deserted even on the weekends, much less on a Thursday night. My heart sank, even as I kicked backwards at him, hoping to land a blow south of the waist.

I got him in the shin instead, not nearly as effective, but enough to raise a "Huh!" of surprise. I shrieked, hoping to add to the din of the horn and addle his brain, but all that did was make him mad. He whopped me upside the head with an open hand. If he'd fisted it, it would have knocked me out or broken my neck, but I guess he wasn't used to victims who actually fought back. He couldn't control both my hands, so I went for his face, hoping to scratch him conspicuously, and I dug in. My nails are always short, so I didn't make as much of a gouge as I'd hoped for, but he was bleeding and cursing up a storm. He hit me again, and this time he did a better job of it.

"Help!" I screamed, and someone actually did.

I had completely forgotten Patricia Bledsoe.

Patricia was dancing behind him with a gun in her hand.

If she shot him, she'd get me.

Before I could give my opinion, she seemed to realize that, too, and turned the gun around in her hand. Holding it by the barrel, she poised herself, and swung the butt with all her might. She connected solidly with his head, right above his right ear. There was an awful little noise, like stepping on wet peanut shells, and then he collapsed in a heap.

We stood there and breathed heavily for a minute, Patricia's chest heaving just as hard as mine.

"Oh, thank you," I babbled. "Oh, Patricia, thank you thank you."

"I've got to get out of here," she said precisely, clipping off her words like they were the end of a cigar.

"Yes, sure."

"What are you going to tell them?"

"I'll make up something, you get gone. I won't tell anyone."

"I believe you," she said, sounding a little surprised.

"He could've hit the corner of that table," I said. "It's wood." I wasn't sure if that would make a difference or not, but it sounded good.

"Better put some blood on the corner, then," Patricia advised. She had her envelope still clutched in her hand, and now she tucked it into her skirt pocket.

"Good luck to you and Jerome," I said, and then Patricia Bledsoe—Anita Defarge—was out of the Lawrenceton Library for the very last time, and over the sound of my car honking, I never heard her pull away.

I had a couple of things to do before I called 911. Feeling my whole face pucker with distaste, I touched my fingers to Will Weir's depressed wound, and I rubbed the blood and hair on the corner of the table nearest him. I thought briefly of trying to move him closer to the table, but I was afraid of screwing up things even more. Better leave it simple.

I didn't think I'd ever concealed a crime before in my life. It was kind of exhilarating. I rinsed my hands off in the employee sink, and then poured some cold coffee that had been sitting in the pot down the drain after the tinged water. I left the pot in the sink.

I dialed 911 on the phone in Patricia's office. While I was there, I checked to make sure everything had been left in order. I wondered what had been in the envelope she'd needed so badly—money? Documents?

Whatever it was, she had saved my life by coming back to get it.

As I waited for the police to come, I wondered what would have happened if Patricia hadn't believed I would keep silent. After all, she'd had a gun in her purse, and she'd showed she wasn't afraid to use it. Then I decided there were paths I didn't need to walk, and that was one of them.

It was actually lucky for me that Will had hit me. By the time the room was swarming with police and emergency and library people, the whole left side of my face was swollen and blackening. The bruising had hardly healed from my mishap in the parking lot. I was going to forget what I really looked like. Blood and saliva had made a track down my chin where a tooth had cut the inside of my cheek. In the face of such graphic evidence, and the letter (which I never got to read all the way through) and Mark Chesney's testimony that Will had tried more than once to get Mark to give him the books to bring to the library, I was home free.

Airlifted to an Atlanta hospital, Will Weir lingered in a coma for four days. Then he died.

I had to endure a lot of silent sympathy from people who were sure a gentle woman like me would be harboring lots of guilt at having indirectly caused a death, even the death of someone who was trying to kill me.

I guess they just didn't know me very well.

* * *

If it ever crossed my mind to tell anyone about Patricia/Anita, I sat on the thought as heavily as I could. I imagined her building a new life somewhere else, but I hoped in this new life she would cut Jerome some slack and let him wear Nikes.

Sam waited three more days, griping loudly about Patricia's inexplicable absence, before he called the police, who weren't too swift about telling the FBI. The FBI hopped right on it, fingerprinted the rental house (which had been cleaned, in the interim, by professional cleaners who'd been hired and paid in cash through the mail), fingerprinted the whole office (though by then the library janitor had done a jim-dandy job of cleaning the desk, under Sam's direction) and questioned the whole staff. In the end, they still weren't a hundred percent sure we'd encountered Anita Defarge.

How did Robin handle all this? After all, he'd been with me when I saw the picture. Somehow Robin realized that identifying Patricia Bledsoe was no high priority of mine. I may have whispered something to him to that effect in the dark of the night, the night I moved into my new house. And since he had his plate full testifying against Tracy, moving his stuff from California to the small house on Oak my mother found for him, and doing some rewrites on the script of *Whimsical Death*, Robin didn't ask any questions.

I like that in a man.

The Crystal Rose

New York Times bestselling author

REBECCA BRANDEWYNE

London, England, 1850: Rose Windermere is nearly knocked to the ground by a man who whispers a dire warning…and presses a letter into her hands before fleeing. The mark with which the letter is sealed recalls Rose's idyllic childhood in India and a world that was destroyed when an uprising left her friend Hugo dead.

Pulled back into the exotic land of her youth, Rose must now unravel the strange machinations of a man whose lust for power will threaten a monarchy—and Rose's own heart.

"Intriguing tale (à la Dickens) that will captivate gothic fans."
—*Romantic Times BOOKreviews*
on *The Ninefold Key*

Available the first week of December 2006,
wherever paperbacks are sold!

www.MIRABooks.com

MRB2296

USA TODAY bestselling author

ANN MAJOR

He always got what he wanted.

Pierce Carver was one of Austin's most successful surgeons. He was going to marry trauma nurse Rose Marie Castle and put her aching feet into glass slippers. But he couldn't give up his womanizing ways, so he jilted Rose Marie....

Then someone wanted him dead.

Things were looking bad for Rose Marie. After her ex was murdered she became the prime suspect. Worse, her high school sweetheart was the investigating detective. But if Rose Marie didn't kill the not-so-good doctor, who did?

THE SECRET LIVES OF DOCTORS' WIVES

"Ann Major's name on the cover instantly
identifies the book as a good read."
—*New York Times* bestselling author Sandra Brown

REQUEST YOUR FREE BOOKS!

2 FREE NOVELS FROM THE ROMANCE/SUSPENSE COLLECTION PLUS 2 FREE GIFTS!

USA TODAY
bestselling author

ANNE STUART

NEVER GET IN THE WAY OF A MISSION.

The job was supposed to be dead easy—hand-deliver
some legal papers to billionaire philanthropist Harry Van
Dorn's extravagant yacht, get his signature and be done. But
Manhattan lawyer Genevieve Spenser realizes she's in the
wrong place at the wrong time when she meets Peter.

Peter Jensen is far more than the unassuming personal assistant
he pretends to be—and Genevieve's presence has thrown a
wrench into his plans. Now he must decide whether to risk
his mission in order to keep her alive, or allow her to become
collateral damage....

COLD AS ICE

"Brilliant characterizations and a suitably moody ambience
drive this dark tale of unlikely love."
—*Publishers Weekly*, starred review, on *Black Ice*

Available the first week of November 2006 wherever paperbacks are sold!